Idumea

# Idumea

x

A Post-Self story

Madison Rye Progress

with contributions from

Samantha Yule Fireheart

Krzysztof "Tomash" Drewniak

ISBN: 978-1-948743-47-1

*Idumea*



This book uses the fonts Gentium Book Basic, Gotu and Linux Biolinum O and was typeset with X$_\exists$LAT$_E$X.

# Post-Self books

The Post-Self Cycle
by Madison Rye Progress (as Madison Scott-Clary)
I. *Qoheleth*
II. *Toledot*
III. *Nevi'im*
IV. *Mitzvot*

*Clade — A Post-Self Anthology*
Various authors

*Unintended Tendencies*
by JL Conway

*Marsh*
by Madison Rye Progress *et al.*

*Motes Played*
by Madison Rye Progress & Samantha Yule Fireheart

*Ask. — An Odist Q&A*
Various authors

*Idumea*
Madison Rye Progress *et al.*

Learn more at *post-self.ink*

**Note:** this book takes place in the Post-Self setting and touches on the plots of The Post-Self Cycle, as well as that of *Marsh*. It is still a standalone novel, but might benefit from having read those works first. They are available as paperbacks, ebooks, and free to read in the browser, and you may find them and much more at *post-self.ink*.

**Content notes:** brief description of sex, themes of self harm, suicide, and poor mental health.

The section with Warmth In Fire on page 91 is a collaboration with Samantha Yule Fireheart.

The section with The Dog and The Rabbit Chaser on page 142 is a collaboration with Krzysztof "Tomash" Drewniak.

Idumea                                                      3


Appendices                                               209


I — Notes · · · · · · · · · · · · · · · · · · · · · · · · 211

II — Ode to the End of Death · · · · · · · · · · · · · 247

III — The hymn "Idumea" · · · · · · · · · · · · · · 255

IV — Reading · · · · · · · · · · · · · · · · · · · 257

# Dramatis Personae

## The Ode clade

Your Humble Narrator
Dear The Wheat And Rye Under The Stars

The Woman
To Pray For The End Of Endings

Her Friend
I Must Show No Hesitation When Speaking My Name

Her Therapist
Where I May Ever Dream

Her Cocladist
Should We Rejoice In The End Of Endings

The Oneirotect
Which Offers Heat And Warmth In Fire

The Instance Artist
Dear, Also, The Tree That Was Felled

The Poet
Where It Watches the Slow Hours Progress

The Musician
Beholden To The Heat Of The Lamps

The Child
And We Are The Motes In The Stage-Lights

The Narrator's Friend
Time Is A Finger Pointing At Itself

The Blue Fairy
I Remember The Rattle Of Dry Grass

<u>Others</u>

Her Lover
**Farai**

The Dog
**Scout Among Weird Skunks With Good Kettlecorn**

His Elder
**Tomash**

The Rabbit-Chaser
|             | **(called "Scout Chasing Rabbits")**

**And, of course, you, my dear, *dear* reader.**

People of Orphalese, beauty is life when life unveils her holy face. But you are life and you are the veil. Beauty is eternity gazing at itself in a mirror. But you are eternity and you are the mirror.

— Kahlil Gibran

End Of Endings — 2403

×

Rye — 2409

×

Once upon a time there was–

"A king?" my little readers will immediately say.

No, children, you are mistaken. Once upon a time, there was a woman. She was not a fine woman, not a prize to adorn your arm or to set beside you at the head of a grand table, but a simple woman—the kind we pass on the street and imagine some plain home life for. She has a house, one might think. There are floors and walls and windows, there are tables and chairs and sofas and beds. There is a shower and a claw-footed bathtub. There is a creaky step—the eighth—that she always swears she will fix.

We must imagine such a woman happy. We must imagine that she has friends and that she goes and drinks okay wine or maybe strange cocktails with them at the most absurd bars. We must imagine that she comes home, wobbling slightly with each step, with some other simple woman on her arm. We must imagine them sharing their kisses, being happy together.

We must imagine these things because they are not true.

I do not know how it happened, but one cloudy day, she was asking after her friend most pure and then her mind was turned all in on itself, was wrapped and folded three times, turned, and then wrapped and folded thrice more. Some malicious baker kneaded and kneaded and kneaded, and when next she woke up, sixteen hours and twenty three minutes later, her mind remained in some unknown, integral way tied up into knots.

But that was three hundred years ago.

×

The Woman wanders the world some few times a month, stepping out into unknown nowheres and known somewheres to be seen, to be perceived as still existing. I do not know why, but it is important to her that someone witness her existing. It is a striving, an aiming for perfection, a ritual she follows around like a little puppy: she will not know what will happen when she first does it properly, but she hopes it will be something wonderful.

The Woman has many rituals.

She has rituals for eating food, for feeding the vessel in which she makes her home. There is no order in which she properly consumes food, she may consume it in any order, but there is an order in which she must appreciate food. You must understand: she has to do this for everything she takes into her body. She must look at it before she touches it, must touch it before she smells it, must smell it before she eats it, and before all of these she must say a prayer.

She has rituals for getting dressed, for clothing the form with which the world sees her. She must choose a garment that fits her body and one that fits her mood. You must understand: every time she gets dressed, there is a moment of scrying into her deepest self and estimating how it is that she feels that day. And should her mood change, should those feelings shift, she will find her clothing itchy and uncomfortable, and if her form becomes not what it once was, her clothing will become uncomfortably tight or perhaps she will disappear down into the folds of fabric.

She has rituals for entering a room, for passing through a door. She must touch the door frame beside her shoulder, must brush her fingers against the wood or stone or metal or some more abstract substance. You must understand: she has to do this for every door she walks through, and for this reason, there is a door in the house where she lives that was built by a friend of Her Friend that leads directly out into a city. She opens the closet door and steps out onto a concrete sidewalk lined with trees and passers-by, where the sun shines bright and the air burns cold in her nostrils and the dry leaves skitter anxiously about her feet. As she steps out, she can brush her hand to the door jamb.

I do not know where these rituals come from, and perhaps some of my readers will immediately say, "OCD? Does The Woman have obsessive compulsive disorder?"

Perhaps she does, perhaps she does not. I do not know, friend. I *do* know that there are obsessions within her, yes, and I am sure that these rituals feel compulsory, but there is something different about The Woman. She is too present. She is too much herself, too human, too embodied within her vessel as it spirals out of control, too stuck in her mind as it twists in on itself. She is less struck by a disorder than she is struck by a constant overwhelm, a constant overflowing.

The Woman uploaded when she was overflowing. She lived within that overflow for years, for twelve years she was overflowing, she was trapped within her mind and within the vessel of her body, and she lived as best she can as her body spiraled out of control.

Readers, you must understand that she was in so many ways whole still!

She campaigned for herself and for the others as damaged as her, but I think this was borne out of trauma and desperation as much as it was care for her loved ones lost and found.

She campaigned after uploading for individual rights for uploaded minds, before they were even cladists, before forking and sensorium messages and all of the other benefits that the System has to offer.

She was whole because she maintained—even while overflowing, I think!—so many deeply held convictions that those around her need not suffer, even if she herself did. Especially, she would say, because she herself did.

I think that she would say, however, that she was *too* whole. I think she would say that she was *too* full, too much, too alive. I think she would say that almost three hundred years of a life that was lived as hers was, with her mind turned in on itself, was too much life. I think she would laugh that hoarse, dry laugh that always sounded like tears were on the way, and say that thirty years was probably too much for her.

×

"I wish," The Woman said some decades after Michelle Hadje who was Sasha uploaded, after she became End Of Endings of the Ode clade, of the tenth stanza, "I wish I could unbecome."

Her Friend frowned and replied, "Do you mean you wish you could die?"

"No, I specifically do not mean that."

"What do you mean by 'unbecome', then?"

"I mean that I wish I could go through the process of becoming backwards."

"I am guessing you do not mean that you wish you could come apart."

The Woman laughed and shook her head. "No, though if I had to line them all up on a scale, I would prefer coming apart to dying. I would just prefer to unbecome more than that."

Her Friend was a good person who always treated The Woman well. Ey knew just how to talk to her, just which questions to ask, just when it was okay to offer a hug and when to hold back. Ey was a therapist of sorts, or at least someone dedicated to understanding the vagaries of the mind, someone who sought ever to reclaim different aspects of a less-than-ideal life, a less-than-ideal past.

"Do you know what that looks like?" Her Friend asked.

"Not yet," The Woman said. "Not yet."

"Is there a time when you will, then?"

"I think so, just not quite yet."

×

Every year, there would be a gathering on her birthday—their birthday, for Her Friend was also of the Ode clade, also of Michelle Hadje who was Sasha—and they would sit somewhere, whether it was out on the porch of the home The Woman shared with the rest of the tenth stanza, or out on the dandelion-speckled lawn, or, once the door had been built into the house, on rickety chairs outside a cafe over identical coffees.

Every time they would meet up thus, The Woman and Her Friend would take a few minutes to themselves to have the same conversation:

Her Friend would ask, "Have you figured out what unbecoming looks like yet, my dear?"

"Not yet," The Woman would say. "Not yet."

"And have you any idea on when you might?"

"Not yet, no."

And then Her Friend would ask The Woman if ey could hug her, and she would usually say yes, for she saved up her energy for these parties, and ey would hug her and lean down to whisper gently beside her ear, "When you do, be sure that you tell me, End Of Endings. I want that you feel good above all things."

"Yes, No Hesitation," she would say. "I want you to be there with me, if ever I figure out just what I mean."

And after that, they would go to the rest of the party at the home of the tenth stanza.

I think you would like to see these parties, friends. I think that they would not be quite as you would expect, of course. They are not the kinds of birthday parties that you or I might have. Where we might have cakes and singing and the blowing out of candles, they would gather together over simple foods—so many from the tenth stanza had such sensitive tastes, and it was so easy to make sure that everyone could eat everything!—and often they would simply sit silent. They would sit there, quiet, but present in each other's company.

They would not seem to be parties like you and I have perhaps because this was not all that different from what might happen once or twice a month at the house in which the tenth stanza all lived. While each lived their own lives, occasionally, their schedules would coincide and they would all sit down together at the giant oak table together and eat, mostly in silence.

Some of them shared rooms, you see, but mostly, they kept to themselves. They lived together in that big Gothic house plopped right down in the middle of a prairie of green grass and yellow dandelions, out where the stoop stepped down directly into the field, but I say 'lived together' in a very mechanical sense. They never shared meals intentionally, nor even spoke all that often to each other. It is just that, sometimes, they would all find themselves at table at the same time!

So the only difference between parties and those days when they all found themselves eating together was mostly that this time, they actually *meant* to, and these were the days when, most often, more than one of them would invite over a friend or a guest.

The Woman invites Her Friend over more than any of the other members of the tenth stanza invite others over, except perhaps back when Should We Forget was alive, and The Oneirotect, my beloved up-tree, would come by to give her little gifts and toys, little trinkets and special snacks that she would divvy up and share with the rest of the stanza in little unlabeled envelopes.

But Should We Forget was no longer alive, not since the world had turned in on itself and had eaten so many of those who lived within, and now that meant that The Woman, out of all of those who lived together, there on the field, brought over company most often.

X

When Michelle who was Sasha had quit, out on a field so sim-ilar to the one that she lived on, The Woman breathed a sigh of relief, because she knew—though I do not think she know how—that Michelle who was Sasha had found her own relief in those last moments. She had looked up to the sky, up to our own personal *HaShem,* up to The Dreamer who dreams the world in which we live, and in those moments she knew relief. She knew relief and she knew joy and she knew so, so much peace.

Peace! That was one of the things that The Woman craved. She wanted nothing more than to know a little bit of peace.

No rituals.

No overflowing.

None of this shifting of form that would strike unawares, for there she would be, sitting as pretty as could be, just this woman, just this short, round woman with a round, pale face and curly, black hair, and then with a cry or with a whimper or with a sigh of defeat, her very form would shift from beneath her. Her conception of herself would slip from her grasp and she would cease to be The Woman and instead be The Skunk or The Pan-ther, for the woman, you see, rather liked these animals. It was always one of those three, for some days, she would be happily The Panther, and then a bee would land on her nose and tickle her whiskers and she would sneeze herself into a skunk.

I think it was cute sometimes, and I think she would say the same. I think she would say, "Oh! Oh! Look at that!" and then she would set to work brushing her tail. After all, what else is one to do if they found themselves to be in possession of such caudal beauty as is a skunk?

This is why The Woman had so much trouble with clothing, you see. She would try to look deep within herself at her moods to see what it is that she felt and how it was that the day might go and she might come up with a pretty skirt that felt good on her legs and a lovely shirt she liked the look of, but then, some time later, the shirt would be puffy with fur and the skirt would not sit right with her tail.

No rituals. No overflowing. Just peace. It is hard to experience peace, hard to experience joy when one is too much oneself, is it not?

×　　×

The Woman decided to go walking one day. Perhaps she was driven by restlessness. She had an errand to run, sure, but this day she decided to go out walking rather than perform this task at home or simply blip into being at her destination. Perhaps she was bored! I do not know.

Either way, she was feeling good and she was feeling stable and she was feeling feline, so she found herself a nice set of slacks to wear over her legs, ones that looped up over the base of her tail in such a way that the same would be just as possible with a skunk's tail, and yet which would not fall down for those moments when she did not have a tail.

She found herself a nice shirt that felt good on the fur and which would not look too weird if she poofed out into a skunk. It was not her favorite shirt, I am sure, otherwise maybe she would wear it every day, but she liked it well enough. It had the word 'fiend' scribbled across it in angular, glitchy graffiti, and The Woman is absolutely allowed to feel like a fiend some days.

Thus gussied, The Woman stood for a while in front of the mirror and admired herself. She felt good. She felt good, reader! It was not often that she felt more than just okay. Because even with all that I wrote about before, her life was not bad. It was an okay life. She liked this life in her own way. Her thoughts on unbecoming were not thoughts on suicide, I do not think.

She stood before the mirror and primped for a moment, adjusting the way her shirt sat and fluffing out her slacks to see how they might fit with a thicker coat. She combed her claws through her short fur to straighten out some mussed-up spots and ensured that her whiskers were all neat and in those rows that cats have that she always found fascinating.

The trip to the city was as it ever was. She said to herself a little prayer and opened the door to her closet. Taking a deep breath, she stepped through, and as she did so, she brushed her fingertips against the jamb as ever, against some imagined *mezuzah,* and today it felt right enough that she stepped lively out onto the city streets, out where the leaves skittered anxiously around her footpaws in the faint February breeze.

Stuffing her paws into her pockets, she made her way down the street on which her entrance was located to the main drag. The city was on the small end—more large town than full on city—and so it was still the type of place to have a main drag, a street built for cars that it does not actually have, with wide sidewalks paved in brick and a trolley that ran down the middle.

The Woman waited for the next trolley car to come and stepped aboard, tucking her tail down and around her leg as she held onto one of the railings—she never sat, and never could tell you why—to ride it for three stops. This was part of the ritual. Even when the car was busy and she was not feeling so good, there was a part of her that was happy that she got to stand on this trolley and hold onto this railing and feel this rattle-buzz of the wheels rolling along the track through her feet or paws.

It was not even particularly pleasant for her, I think, but it *was* fulfilling.

She made it her three stops and stepped easily from the trolley to find herself before her usual coffee shop. There was so much comfort in routine sometimes. Not all routines are rituals, after all, sometimes there was just a coffee shop that you really like because it makes good mochas and always gives you extra whipped cream without being asked.

And so that was just the routine that she engaged with.

Once The Woman had her mocha with extra whip, once she had one of her usual tables over by the windows, once she had taken a seat, then at last she let her shoulders relax, let the tension drain out of the small of her back, let her tail curl around a leg of the chair so that she could simply exist out in public, just sit in her chair by the window and watch the life of the city roll by outside and listen to the rumble-chatter of the coffee shop and, in turn, be watched, be heard, be witnessed.

×

The Woman loved a good mocha—even I love a good mocha!—and so she was plenty happy to go to the coffee shop every now and then to pick one up, to sit by the window and watch and listen to the world go by, but this was not why she is here today. This was not her errand.

That day, The Woman was here because Her Friend had asked to meet up.

This was not how this usually went, you understand. Usually, The Woman was upset and asked for Her Friend to visit her, or perhaps she was out anyway and simply desired company on this errand or that, a friend for dinner or coffee or a walk along the shops to peruse the latest trends in fashion or oneirotecture or sensework. It was so often the case that The Woman contacted Her Friend, and not the other way around.

Her Friend was always so stable, always so ready to speak and so ready to listen. Ey was the one who had long ago gotten in touch with her, with the whole of the tenth stanza, and started to talk to them and listen to what they had to say. Not the only one, no, but it was important to The Woman that Her Friend had sought her out, had cared enough to seek her out.

That had been in the context of learning more about The Woman and her stanza, though. It had been in the context of try-ing to understand what made the tenth stanza the tenth stanza. There had been an offer of help, but a very gentle one. The Woman had been the one to accept that offer, but more than that, Her Friend really did just want to learn, rather than teach, to listen rather than talk.

Her Friend really did just want a friend, too, for the seventh stanza were all friends with each other, she was promised, and yet they had their own struggles. In Dreams was, she was ever promised, eager to help, eager to teach and to learn and to listen and to talk. There was advice to be given and the knowledge of psychology gleaned over however many hundreds of years now on offer—was it really nearly 300? There was-

"End Of Endings?"

"Ah! My dear, my dear," The Woman said, pushing herself to her feet to bow. "A pleasure, a pleasure. Please, sit, if you would like, or I am also happy to walk."

Her Friend smiled faintly, bowed in turn, and pulled out the ratty chair across the table, curled her tail around, and fell into it heavily, eir own identical mocha set before em. "How are you feeling, my dear? Well, I hope?"

Returning to her own seat, The Woman nodded. "Quite well, yes. It was a quiet and comfortable morning, and it was an easy trip here. The house was calm and the coffee shop is calm. How are you, though? You sounded...well, I suppose you sounded uncomfortable. You sounded like you were trying to be quiet."

"I was, yes." Ey laughed, looking sheepish. "I do not know why. I was in a cone of silence. I suppose it must have been a mood thing."

"And how is your mood?"

"That is actually what I wanted to speak with you about."

The Woman furrowed her brow, whiskers and ears both canting back. "*You* wanted to speak with *me* about moods?"

Her Friend leaned forward, resting eir arms on the edge of the table. "Well, I wanted to speak with a friend about my moods, yes? That is what we are, yes? Friends?"

She laughed. "Of course, my dear. You are my best."

Her Friend's smile grew yet more earnest. "Thank you. That feels better to hear than I expected."

"So, tell me of your moods, then. Tell me why you were uncomfortable and felt the need to speak quietly."

"Well," ey began, blinking a cone of silence into being over the table. "I suppose it is In Dreams. It is a few of them, actually."

The Woman nodded, lifted her drink for a sip, sighed. "You have had mostly good things to say of them."

"Mostly, yes."

"But not always."

"Yes." Her Friend turned eir mug lazily from side to side on the tabletop, not yet drinking. "Not always. There are times when we mesh quite well. Most times, even. There are times when we will go out for coffee in the morning and stay together in a group, but there are also times when we will lag behind, me and a few others. There are times when we will all eat together sitting around one table or having a picnic, talking about our days, and there are times when we will retreat to our own homes and eat by ourselves or with our partners."

The Woman averted her eyes, nodded. "As we do."

"As you and yours do, yes," Her Friend said cautiously.

The topic had been fraught for nearly sixty years now. Those meals were lovely, to be sure, as were the times when they would talk or sit in silence together, out there on the field, enjoying warmth and sun or perhaps the light of the moon.

It had not been all of them for sixty years, though. Not since Death Itself had died, her and I Do Not Know. Not since Death Itself had fallen into catatonia and then smiled, shrugged, and quit. Not five hours later, I Do Not Know had sighed comfortably, turned over in her bed, and then quit as well.

Fifty-eight years since the last meal they had all shared together.

Even so, The Woman—her and her whole stanza—insisted for years that it was all of them who ate together, when the remainder of the tenth ate together. *All* of them, all together. They insisted on that, friends, just as they insisted on leaving two empty chairs at the table, two plates of food set before them.

With a deliberate motion of sharp-clawed paws, The Woman drew a definitive line across the table, defining an arc around her. With this, she blocked the topic off, reflected the thoughts of loss and trauma away from herself, out somewhere else. It was a practiced motion, smooth and careful, and one that Her Friend knew well.

Ey nodded, understanding, and continued. "The reasons we might not eat with each other or that some of us may wander away on our outings are varied, of course. There are long-standing shifts in the way the stanza works together, yes? It has been a long time since we have been so alike. Sometimes, however, it is a little thing. One of us will say something that rubs another the wrong way and it will take us time to work it out. We will write our letters or have our conversations and it will be fine in time."

"Is that what happened this time?"

Her Friend hesitated. "Yes," ey said carefully. "I said something to In Dreams, I said that I was feeling unwell, that my stress had been high and that I was worried I might be overflowing—or at least on the brink of such—but also that I was feeling particularly rough about the Attack. I was feeling grief and loss."

The Woman's breath caught in her throat.

When I tell you that breath is important even sys-side, you must understand all of the different roles that it plays. We are built to breathe, you and I, and so is everyone else. We can turn that off, sure, but the vast majority of cladists find such uncomfortable. Not breathing still feels like holding one's breath, yes? Even without the rising $CO_2$ levels in our blood—blood that we must only imagine that we have—it is uncomfortable to feel like one is holding one's breath for too long.

We use breath for speaking, and even though I am not speaking to you right now, I am still breathing. I still feel the warmth of my breath against my paw as it brushes across the page with each line of text. We use breath for gasping, for sighing, for even snoring!

So when I tell you that The Woman's breath caught in her throat, you must imagine the way your breath might catch in your own throat when suddenly you hear something that causes a rising tide of emotions that takes precedence even over that, even over breathing. You must picture the way that you feel when, if you were to breathe, you fear there might be a whine of fear or a moan of terror—or even pleasure, because we are no less susceptible to that.

And here, now, The Woman was feeling most of all grief. She feared that, were she to let her breath out, it would be that whine of fear, that moan of terror, a wave of tears.

The tenth had left two empty chairs and two full plates at meals until three years prior, until the Century Attack.

Now they left three.

Her Friend, either knowing or seeing this, averted eir eyes, casting eir gaze instead out to the street. "I am sorry, my dear. I was indeed feeling grief and loss over Should We Forget. No Longer Myself as well, yes, and Beckoning and Hammersmith and more, but the one I knew best was Should We Forget. I am sorry."

The Woman let her breath out most carefully, not letting it shake, not letting her lip quiver. "I understand, yes. You knew her as well."

"Perhaps we can speak simply of the fallout."

She bowed. "I would appreciate that, yes."

"Of course," Her Friend said, smiling, nodding eir acknowledgement. "The fallout of this conversation with In Dreams was that she told me that perhaps I ought to schedule a session, either with her or In Memory, or, failing that, someone outside the clade."

"Is that what you wound up doing?"

Ey shook eir head. "I did not need that, my dear. I did not need to be told to go to therapy. I did not want to schedule an appointment." Ey finally took a sip of eir mocha, but this seemed to be less about the coffee than an opportunity to gather eir thoughts. "I just wanted a friend, honestly. I just wanted a hug—no, I understand, perhaps not your thing, but I must be earnest, yes? Instead, I got told to find a way to *fix* this. Fix grief. Fix a very real pain."

The Woman's features softened and, steeling herself for the touch, she reached across the table to pat the back of Her Friend's paw. "I understand, No Hesitation. Would that I could offer more. I am happy to be a friend, though; I have no interest in telling you to go to therapy."

"Of course," ey said, smiling once more. "I trust you of all people in that. I know that you have mentioned—however kindly—in the past that you have worried that I am simply providing you with therapy on the sly, but I trust that you know that such is not the nature of our friendship."

She nodded.

"All I wanted was to be close to someone who would not do those things."

"Yes, of course. There are many memories bound up in all of this, but there is also joy, yes? Joy that we are still here? That is what I have been trying to focus on."

"Oh? How so?"

"I do not know how healthy it is to treat those who are lost as if they are still there, but I also do not know that this is what I am doing. I do not even know if that is what the others are doing, yes? They might very well be, given the open seats on the table that we leave, given the conversations I hear at night from my cocladists. Rejoice speaks with Death Itself in quiet whispers while laying in bed. Many of them talk with RJ, still. I myself have talked with Michelle and Sasha, when I remember days long ago on her field, listening to her speak of being a dead woman walking when she was having bad days or gushing about Debarre on her good ones. Many of us speak to the dead."

Her friend furrowed eir brow. "Do you want my opinion as a friend, or do you want my opinion as a therapist?"

The Woman shrugged.

"As a therapist, I would say that there is such a thing as an unhealthy attachment, that holding onto past traumas makes it awfully easy to reinflict them on oneself." Her expression shifted kind as she continued. "As your friend, I would say that, if that helps, if there is, as you say, joy in it, then by all means, continue. If you can pray to the dead to feel joy, then perhaps you must."

"I see," she said, buying herself a moment to think by sipping her mocha. Ah, but she was a cat, yes? A panther? Perhaps you can imagine this with lapping tongue, the way a cat's tongue curls back and scoops up drink, drawing it up into their mouth. Or perhaps she is the type who has leaned into another aesthetic, the type who can chew with her mouth closed. Idle distractions, even for your humble narrator. "Then yes, there is joy in it. There is joy in those memories, is there not? One takes a moment of stillness…"

After a long few seconds of silence, Her Friend tilted eir head. "Yes?"

"Ah, a fleeting thought. One takes a moment of stillness and parks in that quiet joy, even if it is one of separation."

"Is there joy in loss?"

"I do not know. Is there?"

Her Friend laughed, shaking eir head and leaning back with mocha in hand. "This is what I needed, my dear. I needed to speak with a friend. I needed chat about memories and watching the way you smile when you talk even about these sad things, not sitting on some therapist's couch for the third time in as many weeks."

The Woman preened. This, you see, is more than just a brushing out of imperfections, but a shift in attitude. When The Woman preened—when her whole clade preened, even!— she would sit up a little straighter with a subtle shimmy, lift her snout, close her eyes, bristle her whiskers, and smile a smile that was just south of smug. It is *very* cute, reader, I can assure you of that.

They fell then into comfortable chatter over just the small things: the coffee, the weather, the chairs and how they were *almost* comfortable, but not quite. They fell into warmth and companionship, and all the while, the woman set that fleeting thought she had had just off to the side, where she could keep track of it without it distracting.

Perhaps this unbecoming that her mind circled around was simply the utmost in stillness.

×

The Woman rode the high of lovely friendship for days after that coffee date. For nearly a week, she reveled in the sense of camaraderie and coexistence. How lucky she was! How lucky that she had the chance to exist in the same universe as Her Friend! How lucky, how lucky.

Whenever The Woman felt this way, she would wander around the house and clean. She would take on extra cooking duties and make extra desserts for her cocladists and their friends. She would stay in one form for far longer than was her usual, and remained now a panther. She would go for walks around the field, treating the house itself as a signpost at the center of widening circles. She would imagine that those circles might some day spread out across the entire world, never mind the varied infinities housed within the field itself. It was a thing to which she could give herself as she asked her high-minded questions: am I a falcon, a storm, or a great song?

These words of Rilke's would dance unblushing through her mind, linking arms on one side with the words of Dickinson which ever twined around those of her clade—*If I should die, And you should live, And time should gurgle on, And morn should beam, And noon should burn, As it has usual done...*—and on the other with the lingering lines of the Ode that made up the names of her clade. "I remember the rattle of dry grass," she would explain to the bees as they buzzed in friendship around her ankles. "I remember the names of all things and forget them only when I wake."

And so she would cook her meals and walk in widening circles around this primordial tower that was her home, perhaps circling around God, though she did not care one way or the other if there was that of God in everything.

These were her joys to go along with the needs of ritual, of brushing her fingers along imagined *mezuzot*. To walk was her ritual, to spiral outward from her home in the warmth of sunlight and the dance of bees and the tickling of dandelions against her ankles was to cast that ritual in the light of pleasure.

I have never been quite so fond of walking, myself, kind readers. There is meditation in it, I am told. I am told there is the simple pleasure of the one-foot-in-front-of-the-other-ness of it. But friends, I am tired most of the time. I am old and I am tired and my pleasure lies in stillness and quiet. I love my mochas and I love sitting down before the page with pen in paw to put to paper and I love bathing in story.

I say so often that stepping away from such a task is still writing. When I sit on the patio in front of our little bundle of townhouses and look out at the shared lawn, or when I step—*stepped,* for it is no longer here—out to the shortgrass prairie of my cocladist, to sit beside a cairn of stones or share a meal, that is still writing! Your narrator has written these words, this story, a hundred, a thousand times within her head. That is my joy, and graphomania my compulsion.

When The Woman overflows, she becomes ever more herself. She is—my attentive readers will remember this, of course— she is already too much herself, too whole, too present. This is the nature of overflowing, you see: we become so much ourselves that it begins to ache, to press at our chest from the inside. For your humble narrator, that graphomania strikes with

such force that meaning falls away from my words only gibber-
ish comes forth, or perhaps I will write the same phrase over and
over and over, unable to sate my own compulsions.

My astute readers will surely have picked up by now that I
am riding that edge here, in these words.

But, ah–! This story is not about me. I am not quite overflowing yet, and The Woman most certainly is not. She is reveling in
the warmth of sunlight and the dance of bees and the tickling
of dandelions against her ankles and the purringly soft touch of
friendship.

×

×   ×

The turn away from joy was slow and, at first, unnoticeable.

The Woman did all that she could to hang onto joy whenever it slipped into her life. We all do, do we not? When I find a bakery that serves delectable treats, for instance, I will eat in the tiniest bites I can get away with—nearly crumbs!—just to let the joy of such a treat linger longer on my tongue. The woman did this with her own joy, you see: she would cook these lovely desserts for herself and her cocladists that she might store up joy in carefully sweetened and delicately decorated cupcakes or muffins or cookies or brownies. Joy, it seems, is stored in the chocolate, and so she doles that out to those who deserve joy—and The Woman knows that even she deserves joy.

But even like me with my little tasty baked treats, The Woman's joy is parceled out bit by bit to herself and her cocladists and, just like my little plates of carrot cake—I *do* love a good carrot cake!—there is never an infinite amount, much as she might wish, nor, it always seems, quite enough.

She hung onto joy and baked her goodies and went for her walks and awaited, with some trepidation, her regularly scheduled therapy, because I think she knew that, being confronted with recounting emotions of the past or discussing emotions to come, her grasp on joy would be tested. Once every two weeks, unless she was overflowing, unless she was in pain, unless she simply could not bring herself to go, The Woman had an appointment for therapy, and she knew there was good to be had in it, for it had proven its use time and again over the years, and yet it was a time for threshing, for harrowing. It was a time for throwing herself at the Work at one level of remove and watching the chaff fall away and the fruits of her labor lay exposed. It was a time for dragging the implements of tools dialectical and behaviors cognitive through the dirt of her to break up into clods her varied neuroses.

But as it goes, as it always goes, the morsels of joy meted gladly out soon began to run dry and the sense of happiness that she felt waned, and those truly *good* days began to fade once more into merely okay.

It was the day of her appointment that The Woman sat up in her bed, bleary-eyed, and looked around her, around her plain and simple room with her plain and simple sheets and plain and simple clothes folded neatly atop a plain and simple chair, ready for wear, and at last sighed, wondering, *Where is it that my joy has gone? Where has it gone?*

Today was therapy, and her joy was gone.

There was no relief within her then. There were no thoughts of, ah, today is therapy! Today she would get to talk to Her Therapist! Today she would get to explore this idea of a joy meted out slowly until it was nothing.

In fact, I would say that there was perhaps even a sort of

protectiveness. I think that she felt some sort of ownership of this concept. I think that she felt like this ending of joy was hers and hers alone. Something to keep to herself until perhaps, some day, she might share it and become still at last, or perhaps even beyond then. It was hers to set before herself and admire or loathe. It was hers to wrap up in pretty paper or hide away in the back of a drawer. I think she may have felt jealousy.

And so it was that The Woman, today a human, today, as ever, dressed comfortably, made herself a peanut butter and banana sandwich with the crusts cut off and poured herself a glass of soy milk and walked out into the field outside her house. She had to balance her sandwich atop her drink in order to complete the ritual of passing through the front door, but she had done this countless times before.

The table and chairs sat nearly a mile out from the tenth stanza's house, sprouting senselessly from the grass as easy and carefree as yet more dandelions. A simple square table with two chairs set before adjacent sides so that she need not look Her Therapist in the eye if she did not want to, so that they might each stare out into some similar distance, so that they may feel companionship, though The Woman never could explain how that worked.

And so The Woman, today a human, walked the mile to the table and sat down with her glass of soy milk and began to eat her sandwich. When, at last, there were only two bites left and the glass was half empty, she sent a delicate ping to Her Therapist, who appeared beside the table, paws folded and kind smile on her face. The visage of a skunk lasted no longer than a second before, with a rapid fork, a human stood before her—for Her

Therapist endeavored always to mirror her species lest she influence The Woman's own, though she leaned far harder into gender-play, and one would be hard pressed to not also see her as a young man—and bowed, then pulled out the chair beside her and sat down.

"I will be finished in a moment, Ever Dream," The Woman said just as she did every session. "Just a few bites left."

"Of course, End Of Endings," Her Therapist echoed in the time-honored ritual. "Please, take your time."

The Woman gave a hint of a bow and enjoyed the last two bites of her sandwich as well as she was able, following each with a sip of soy milk, all while Her Therapist made herself comfortable, sitting back in her chair and gazing out over the field of grass and dandelions, a half-smile on her face.

When at last she dusted her hands free of imagined crumbs, The Woman sat back in her own chair, her cold drink held in both hands—she, like me, enjoys that she can create a drink that stays at precisely the most delicious temperature—Her Therapist smiled and nodded. "Tell me, my dear, how are you feeling?"

"I am feeling alright. I have been cleaning and cooking. I have been going out on walks and stepping away from the sim. I spoke with my friend for several hours some days back, and that provided me with comfort and joy."

"That is delightful to hear," Her Therapist said. "Can you tell me of this joy? I love to hear what it is that makes you happy."

The Woman thought long on this. I would like to imagine she was turning her thoughts on jealousy and protectiveness over and over within her head, investigating them like some bauble, searching for cracks or imperfections, or simply admiring how the mirror-like surfaces never picked up her fingerprints. I think perhaps she was trying to derive the formulae that describe their shapes so that she could better understand them. I think, also, that she had to do her best to suppress a wince.

"Was it a complex sort of joy, End Of Endings?"

She sipped her soy milk in an attempt to maintain control over herself, as sometimes all you need is a thing that you can do deliberately. "It is, yes. It is a joy to see one's friends, is it not? To give energy and to receive in turn? We sat down at our favorite coffee shop and chatted about this and that. We talked of empty chairs at the table. We talked of moods and therapy. I believe– yes?"

Her therapist lowered her hand from where she had raised it. "I do not know No Hesitation as well as I might, for which I feel some regret, but In Dreams confided with In Memory, and my down-tree confided in me that she had some fears that she had offended em. Given the structure of our stanza, I think it perhaps unwise that I know too much of that particular conversation until No Hesitation speaks to me emself."

The Woman lingered again in silence, and her mind was aswirl with undefined thoughts that she could no longer pin down, and where once she felt alright, she began to feel something far more tentative, and where once there was a bauble of thoughts on joy, there was now some rectilinear ember, sharp-edged, that she no longer wished to behold, which she quickly dropped and stepped away from in fear and in pain.

"Yes, Ever Dream. Of course. I will speak of other things."

And so they did. It was not an unproductive therapy session, and perhaps Her Therapist was even right. The seventh stanza was as they were, yes? They were the types to go out for coffee together, to eat together, to live as neighbors. The Woman did not know whether Her Therapist lived among them, but at this point, she supposed that she must, should such a prohibition be warranted.

And so they did! They talked of other things, and The Woman did wind up sharing more about her joy, but only in the small ways. She discussed the feeling of making treats for those around her, of storing a little bit of her joy in each—though I believe she left out her feelings on that meting of joy being a depleting—and the ways in which a service such as that which she provided for her own household is a goodness in its own right, is an active participation in joy.

But all throughout, laying at her feet was an ember smoldering, a little cube with edges that could cut as quickly as they could burn, and though she was able to remain present for the remainder of her appointment, was able to remain human, was able to smile and bow to Her Therapist, The Woman was never wholly there, as all throughout, her gaze kept dropping to where at her feet lay an ember smoldering.

X

After therapy, after Her Therapist had left and the chairs had been set beneath the table once more, after a long moment spent standing in the grass with her head hung low, The Woman waved away her empty glass and trudged back to the house.

There was a sense of falling-short within her, a sense of not meeting expectations. Perhaps it was a sense of shame that she had been so keen to hide this idea that she had happened upon, to keep the idea of the end of joy to herself. Perhaps it was because she had so easily let herself be talked out of sharing earnestly that which she would most liked to have discussed. Perhaps it was because—and here I am using words she herself would use—it was because she was a coward. Perhaps, when confronted with something that she believed to be worth talking about, to have such stopped before she could do so took the wind out of her sails, and she was too cowardly to do anything but let that happen. So many perhapses.

It was with these thoughts and these feelings filling her mind to overfull that The Woman walked back to the house, back up the stairs to the porch, back through the door with a brush of fingers on jamb, back up the staircase, back to her room where she stripped and climbed back into bed.

There she slept, and perhaps there she dreamed.

The Woman is a professional in napping in a way that I am not. Perhaps it is the felinity in her, or perhaps it is that she is not so easily claimed by such compulsions as I have— graphomania! Hah!—which lead to such fervent activity. Were I a smarter skunk, I might say to myself: "Rye, my dear, perhaps you can write your novels when you are caught in such throes, and spend the months between practicing the fine art of napping!" But I am not a smart skunk. I am a simple beast who is single minded. I am an animal who does one thing and perhaps does it well. I do not know! I am perhaps too simple to disambiguate between doing a thing well and doing a lot of a thing.

Ah, but perhaps this is why I interpret The Woman at being a professional napper.

Either way, when she returned home and lay down, she immediately fell into a deep, deep slumber. It was a sleep of no dreams, nor perhaps even rest, but served well as a way to disconnect from contexts innumerable, to step away from the world unpleasant. She slept and slept and slept—and yet, she slept for only twenty minutes. Twenty minutes later, she opened her eyes and looked up to the ceiling, and spent another ten minutes picking out familiar patterns in the drywall texture beneath the paint. They were her familiar constellations. There! The fennec. There! The open hand. There! There! There! The swan and the cat and the light-footed opossum dancing around the maypole.

And then, at last, she stood up, and as her feet touched the ground she was, yes, whisked away into felinity, and so it was The Woman who was a cat who padded back downstairs, dressed now in billowy slacks and a flowing blouse. She dressed this way because she felt unstable, and knew that chances were better than not that she would wind up a skunk by that evening.

The living room was empty, but sitting on a stool in the kitchen with a thoughtful expression on her face was Her Cocladist. Her Cocladist, for reasons too complicated for me to pick apart in a fairytale, struggled with her form more even than The Woman did. The Woman would occasionally blip from human to feline or from feline to skunk or from skunk to human, but, in ways that neither I nor The Woman remembered with fondness, Her cocladist lived in a constant superposition of forms. As she sat there on her stool, cheek resting in her palm while a pot bubbled lazily away on the stove, she wisped steadily between skunk and human. Skunk. Human. Skunk. Human. Her pale white skin, which had ever been so soft to the touch and borne such overwhelmingly kind smiles, would give way to black fur. Her hair, curly and dark that framed her face so well, would ghost into a tousled white mane. Behind her a luxurious tail would swish into being and then out again without a second thought.

I do mean that, friends. There is no thought behind this constant changing. When I experienced that, so many years ago, nearly three centuries ago, it was never a thing I could control, not well. I could swallow down a form for a while. I could gulp dryly and linger for a while in humanity, only for a cough or hiccup to come along and send little cookie ears to sprouting, send a white-striped-black muzzle stretching in front of my face.

And always when this happened, the slightest touch would lead to bile rising in my throat. It would feel like sunburn. It would feel like some awful beast letting its bulk settle against me, reminding me of its presence—a threat—with slow breaths.

I do not know if you have ever touched a skunk, dear readers, but they are not silky soft. Their fur is *soft*, yes, but in the plush, cushy way that a dog's might be, or perhaps a short-haired cat. We are truly lovely to pet, I can assure you of that! Why, I will pet my tail for hours as I sit and think and write in my head. In fact, I am doing that right this very minute!

Skunks, I mean to say, are still lovely to pet. We can push our snouts up into your hands and tilt our heads to ensure you scratch in just the right spot behind one ear or another. More, we deserve that. All creatures deserve that which they cherish, and we cherish touch.

We all cherish touch, and in those moments when we were ghosting back and forth, when touch led to vertigo, that which we cherish was taken from us, and for some of us, for The

Woman's cocladist, this was still true. It was not perhaps always true—perhaps there were stretches when she was able to settle into one form and exist in comfort and get gentle, doting pets from The Woman or some other cocladist or some perhaps lover, and perhaps she may yet still.

But for so much of her life, this lovely touch, this cherished thing, was out of reach for Her Cocladist, and so she sat on the stool before the stove while a pot bubbled lazily away.

"Rejoice," The Woman said quietly from the entrance to the kitchen, bowing to Her Cocladist.

Tired eyes swung around to meet her, and an equally tired smile graced both human face and skunk muzzle. "Ah, End Of Endings, my dear, my dear," Her cocladist said twice over. "Have you been well? Have you had a good nap? Did you have a productive therapy session?"

The Woman smiled as well—though her smile was not quite so tired, you understand; she just had her nap—and willed a stool into being some few feet away from Her Cocladist. "I have been well, yes, and my nap was as lovely as always. As for therapy, well..." She trailed off, shrugged.

Her Cocladist nodded. "I understand. I ought to perhaps consider picking such things back up once more. There are many therapists, yes? Not just within our own clade, yes? Perhaps I will seek one of them out some day when I am not so tired."

The Woman nodded. She knew what was coming next, but we all have our rituals, yes?

"But when will that be? Who knows. I am always tired, yes?" A dry chuckle, and then, "Such is our lot in life."

"Perhaps, Rejoice. I would like to think that there is something else. I have been thinking again on the process of unbecoming."

Her Cocladist sat up straighter. "Ah, yes, your dream."

The Woman nodded.

"You will have to tell me when you figure out what that is," Her Cocladist said, then returned to watching the pot. "That is, I think, something that I would be interested in, yes?" She waved a paw that was now a hand that was now a paw again demonstratively.

"Of course, my dear."

Once more, Her Cocladist rested her cheek carefully on her hand or paw or perhaps both. "If there is aught else aside from our lot in life, I would desperately like to know. I am not sure I believe that there is. If the seventh stanza exists to provide us with therapy, then we exist to give them clients. If they need suffering to fix, then we must suffer."

The Woman sat in silence along with Her Cocladist after that, and the house was as as silent as it ever was, and the only noise in the kitchen was the lazy bubbling of a pot on the stove wafting the scent of some mild curry throughout the kitchen, and The Woman wrapped herself up in that scent and took what comfort she could from it as she thought on Her Friend's words some days ago, all but confirming Her Cocladist's sentiment about the seventh stanza, and what it meant that such might also be true for her stanza, the tenth, and her thoughts bubbled as lazily as the pot on the stove and The Woman sat in that silence with Her Cocladist, and the house was as silent as it ever was.

The Woman lingered long on the words of Her Cocladist: *aught else aside from our lot in life.*

What *was* her lot in life? What was *a* lot in life? Was she limited only to one thing? Was she bound to stasis? And what, then, did it mean that a seed had been planted within her and had lately begun to sprout? What of her thoughts on eternal stillness?

She knew where they came from.

Her lot in life had at one point been to teach, to revel in the joy of acting and directing and sets and props and lights and sound and audience and her lovely, loving students who ached for nothing more than to be seen, to receive some perhaps hug from this person who they trusted and yet who could not give them such for fear of pandemic and regulation in equal measure, to receive some perhaps affection from their cohort and yet which their beloved teacher stopped them—was required to stop them—for fear of pandemic and regulation in unequal measure.

She knew the helplessness of having her agency ripped from

her. She knew the feeling of being seen by something larger than mere personhood, a thing which saw her and said, "this here is a wretched and despicable thing," and then took her from the world. And then her lot in life was to campaign, for though she still taught on occasion, still directed, she found she could not act as she wished, and still she had to refrain from hugging for fear of the discomfort of touch.

She knew the feeling of splitting herself into ten unequal parts so that she might at last rest. She knew that her lot in life then became to process what she had become, for that was the role *she* remembered of the tenth stanza, not simply to linger in suffering, but to find a way forward.

She lingered on these thoughts in her unjoy and pondered the meaning, the actions implied, and, with as firm a resolve as a woman who is too much herself could muster, decided that she would *not* lean into this idea of perpetuity as Her Cocladist dwelt within. She may have a lot in life for a time—for a year, for a decade, for a century—but not for the entirety of her existence.

It was within this lingering that she reached out to Her Friend: *"No Hesitation, would you like to meet for coffee? I have something I would like to speak with you about."*

There was a sensation of a tilted head, of a quiet *huh*, in the sensorium message. *"Of course, my dear. So soon after our last meeting, too. I am curious what has you reaching out. When would you like to meet?"*

*"Now, if you are free."*

A laugh, and then, *"I can be. I can send a fork. Same place?"*

*"Yes, please."*

Today, for the first time in she did not know how many years,

The Woman passed through her secret door onto the street with a brush of her fingers on jamb, and then walked to the coffee shop.

*Walked!*

She skipped the trolley! She let go of a ritual, gently set it down on the corner of the street where usually the trolley made its stop, and stuffed her paws in her pockets—for today was a day where she was apparently to be a skunk—and walked briskly to the coffee shop. Yes, the trolley passed her, yes she could have arrived much sooner, but there were the cobblestones beneath her feet-paws and there were the fallen leaves skittering anxiously about her and there was a gentle breeze tugging plaintively at her skirt and her shirt and her mane and her whiskers.

The Woman instructed herself to take joy in these things; or, if not joy, at least pleasure. She tried to feel the seams of cobblestones beneath her unclad feet for a block. She counted leaves for a block. She imagined the wind as gentle paws ensuring that she knew the bounds of her body for the last block. As she opened the door to the coffee shop, she considered her various success and failures in the exercise. The cobblestones were perhaps too cold, but the sensation more pleasing than she had imagined. The leaves made her anxious in turn, but she imagined them having errands to run, their purpose before them. The wind proved to her just how thin her clothing was, and just how thin the fur beneath that was on her chest and belly, but it did indeed remind her of her bounds.

As her fingers brushed over the frame of the door and it shut behind her, she looked over to the bar to find Her Friend ordering the usual two mochas, tail looking quite frazzled.

I do not remember if I told you, dear readers, but The Woman's friend was *also* a skunk. Ey, along with eir stanza, had leaned firmly into that remembered identity. For, you see, we were furries before we uploaded, and we remain always furries. Even those who present as humans—plain and boring! Plain and lovely!—still have that identity within them; metafurry, we have called it. Before we uploaded, before we arrived sysside, Michelle Hadje who was Sasha spent all the time she could online, on the 'net, where she presented herself as Sasha, a skunk who dressed herself in a linen tunic and Thai fisherman's trousers. Prior to that, she had been a panther, too, a feline creature of dark pelt and flowing dresses she never was brave enough to wear as Michelle.

This is the reason why The Woman was at times a skunk and at times a panther and at times a human, and why Her Friend and I are skunks. We remember being a human and then going online to share in our zoomorphic joys with those around us.

And so there as Her Friend, standing by the counter, trying to quickly brush out the frazzled fur of eir tail while the barista worked on the two mochas. On spotting The Woman, though, ey straightened up, smiled, and bowed. "End Of Endings. It is a pleasure to see you again."

The Woman bowed in turn. "Very much so, No Hesitation. Shall I find us a table?"

Her Friend nodded.

The Woman had no trouble in staking out her usual spot, as when one goes to a coffee shop in the middle of the afternoon, there are not quite so many who are hunting down drinks to help them wake up. That is not to say that there is any wrong time for a mocha, mind. I have mine right here, and I am writing this at nearly three in the morning.

"Now," Her Friend said after settling in in eir usual chair. "Tell me how you are feeling. Tell me about this topic you wanted to address."

The Woman smiled. "I am feeling okay. I was feeling quite good after our last meeting, though that faded over time, and for some days, I was feeling rather bad."

Her Friend nodded. "You have mentioned such in the past, yes."

"I suppose I have. I was thinking this time about how I felt so much joy, and how I wanted to share that with my cocladists, so I started making them little treats. It felt like I was putting a little bit of joy into each, though, and that led to me running out."

"Oh? Is this a new thought?"

The Woman furrowed her brow. "Perhaps, yes. I was thinking about it during the lead-up to therapy. I was having several complicated feelings, actually." She laughed, shaking her head. "I was feeling a protectiveness over that. I feel comfortable sharing it with you, my dear, but I did not feel that way with Ever Dream."

"Can you tell me about that?" Ey smiled, adding, "Sorry. I try to stay away from therapeutic language in our discussions, but habits are habits. I really do just want to hear."

"I trust you, No Hesitation." The Woman brushed the longer fur of her mane out her eyes as she pieced together her words. "It felt like a thing to bear within me. I...well, I had considered sharing it, as well, but then Ever Dream requested that I stop. I told her of our meeting and the joy and was going to mention this sharing of joy, but I mentioned our conversation and she stopped me. She said that she would like to hear about it from you herself rather than from me."

Her Friend sighed. "She did not need to maintain confidentiality. I understand why, but she did not need to. I believe that I am your friend before I am her cocladist, but I do not think that she would agree with that."

The Woman sat back in her seat, mocha clutched in her paws. "Alright. I believe you on that, too."

"Did you wish to talk about that? About joy diminishing?"

"No. I wanted to talk about a conversation that came up after the fact. I spoke with Rejoice, and she said that she felt that we are stuck with a joyless lot in life, but the more I think about it, the less I believe that. We may have a lot we are dealt for a portion of our life, but not the whole of it."

"Are you thinking of your unbecoming, then?"

The Woman lapped at her whipped cream for a moment, considering. *Was* she? Perhaps she was. She had not connected those particular dots, but when it was stated aloud by someone other than herself, she felt truth in the worlds. "I suppose I am. I am wondering if reaching for something would be a sort of unbecoming of this static self."

"Ah! That does make sense," Her Friend said, smiling. "If becoming something new means unbecoming your current self, then I will gladly cheer you on, End Of Endings. You are one of my best friends on the System, and so I am happy to see you become ever more what you can be."

The two skunks smiled wide to each other, sharing in this sentiment, this mood, this, yes, joy. The Woman felt it now. She felt that the energy was perhaps not quite there, that she would have to truly exert herself, but that she could still reach for good things in her life. She would have to teach herself joy, and perhaps it would be much like what she had done on the walk here, a presentness or a deliberateness.

The Woman and Her Friend set to work, then, discussing what she could do, what she could learn, what she could yet become.

X

The Woman and Her Friend decided that her path forward would be one of intent and deliberate action. After all, that is how our System works, yes? We intend to be wearing a piece of clothing we like and we are. We intend to step from this sim to that, and we do. We intend to fork and, lo! There beside us stands another instance of ourself! They are a whole new us! They can live their own life, going their own separate way and making their own choices, or perhaps they can go out to do some task or another or visit some friend for coffee and then quit, merging themself—along with all of their memories—back down into us.

They decided on a list of five things that she should try.

Why five, you ask? Well, I honestly do not know! Perhaps because of the five fingers we have on each paw. Perhaps it is because we have two arms, two legs, and a head protruding from our trunk. Or perhaps it has to do with the stars. Starfish? Little wandering doodles to replace the tittles above our 'i's and jots above our 'j's? Each an iota, a mote, a symbol to our future selves, a note for later. Asterisms and asterisks. Footnotes of self.

Ah, but I digress. The Woman and her friend chose a list of five things that she would try—*would*, yes, for *should*, you see, is a value judgment—in order to seek joy in small ways or in small places. The Woman knew that it would be hard. She knew that she would have to bundle up all of her energy and all of her patience with herself and all of her drive and use that to let her last through these explorations of joy.

The first of these five was easy enough to do by herself. She decided first to try new foods. She decided that she would try all *kinds* of foods! She rooted around through the exchange to see what things she had never tried, whether because she was not brave enough or because it sounded like it would taste too strong or because she remembered not liking it back when she was Michelle, back before she had uploaded.

The whole of the clade is, in so many different ways, focused on hedonism. Such is the joy of maintaining a hyperfixation of sorts. That the tenth stanza seemed to have, each at their own point in time, let that hyperfixation on processing shift into a sort of stasis was an accident. None of them are so sad, of course, that they cannot still feel joy in their lives, as we have well seen. The Woman has shown us, yes, and even Her Cocladist, who held so poor a view of her lot in life had joys, for it was her who most often cooked to the peculiar tastes of her stanza.

And The Woman had her own particularities when it came to food. When she cut the crusts off her sandwiches, it was a way to ensure that each bite contained precisely what she wanted in the ratio of bread to filling. After all, one cannot always spread the fillings up to the edge of the sandwich! If you do, your fingers will wind up sticky with peanut butter or mayonnaise and the oil it stains your fur with will leave behind a lasting scent—ask me how I know!—but if you do not, then you wind up with a whole mouthful of little else but bread. It is a balancing act and The Woman has found that if she spreads the peanut butter or mayonnaise just so, then cuts the crusts off, she winds up with more perfect bites than not.

Particularities and peculiarities! The Woman has as many as you or I, dear reader, and perhaps more, and so her first task was to seek that which her particularities and peculiarities had covered up. Was there a thing that she had missed? Was there a food that she had only ever tried bad approximations of and actually earnestly liked?

Yes and no, as is ever the case.

Yes, because, although her spice tolerance was quite low, her flavor tolerance was far higher than she had ever given herself credit for. She found in a Laotian restaurant a salad made with green papaya and soy sauce and fish sauce and mint and cilantro and the crispest lettuce leaves she had ever had a love of a new food. It was so *salty!* It was so *savory!* And yet it sat light on the tongue as mephit teeth struggled to crunch down on the slivers of unripe fruit well enough to macerate. It was sour with lime and tingling in the mouth with mint and coated the tongue with that pleasant soapiness cilantro seems so keen to provide.

The Woman fell in love immediately, and although the tom kha gai that followed was too spicy for her, she plowed through that as well, and set aside the sense of fullness as she worked next on mok pa, a dish of fish served steamed in banana leaves, and finished with a delightful plate of mango and sweet sticky rice, all drizzled with sweetened condensed milk. The fish was lovely, yes, and the dessert delicious, though it stuck in her teeth.

And no, because with each success shining as bright as that crunchy and flavorful tam mak hoong, there were dozens of nights of upset stomachs and burning taste buds. Pineapple, she found, was the fruit that ate you back. Chilies, she found, burned as hot as ever, and there were no ways in which she could comfortably consume them without being left in tears—she was left sobbing, my dears! On one memorable occasion, she was left sobbing, even after she forked with a clean mouth, even then, the remembered pain left her curled in a ball in the back room of the restaurant while the kindly owner doted on her with offerings of ice cream and soft pets and gentle, cooed reassurances.

No, because her limits were reinforced. For every victory, there was a reminder that she was unwhole. My friends, I think that *everyone* is unwhole. I know that I am. I know that I write and write and write, and that is lovely, yes, but I also know that I can be a prickly little terror when caught up in my emotions. I know that I spend my time at my books, at my desk, and, though I try to be a comfortable and comforting presence within my stanza, though I try to dote on my up-tree, I am never able to give quite as much as I would like. I think everyone is unwhole, and I think as well that our unwhole-ness is more evident, more dire to us than it is to those around us. You and I, friends, we see The Woman coming across a boundary in her tastes and nod and think to ourselves, "This is no moral failing! The Woman has done no wrong. She should feel no shame." But to her, it felt like a failure to reach joy.

She, too, understands dialectics, do not get me wrong. She,

too, knows that these reassurances of boundaries also come with the discoveries that she made, all of the green papaya salads and savory Artemisian treats that The Oneirotect, my beloved up-tree, and its ilk had set on the market that she fell in love with. But always before her was the goal of joy, and while she would count her successes, she would also count her failures—no, no, do not contradict her, she saw them as failures and there is now no changing of her mind, not these many years later, not as she is now—and cluck her tongue and shake her head and go home and lay down in her bed and take one of those naps that she was so good at.

There was joy, yes, but it was not a complete joy. Her hedonism with food was a lovely hedonism and she cherished it, but it was not the hedonism she needed for this task.

×

There was no simple way to approach this next attempt at joy for The Woman.

There had been times within her life where she struggled with touch, for when one is too much oneself, every touch is all that much more intense. When one is full to overflowing, each touch runs the risk of oversaturating sensation, pushing a gentle caress into the grating drag of sand over skin.

And yet touch remained important to her. It remains important to all of us! Even I, who surround myself in words, constructs blankets of ink to wrap myself up in, even I relish my time spent with my cocladists and with my friends. I relish the time I spend with My Friend and how, on occasion, we will go for a walk and she will take my paw in her hand in companionship.

Touch remained important to her and, to her, those moments when she was able to accept a hug from her friend shined bright in her memories when she hunted for this next form of joy.

"If," she reasoned to Her Friend over their mochas, "if so many have found joy in touch and sensuality and sexuality, might not I?"

"You may very well, yes," ey said, smiling. "What do you think you will do?"

"I am not sure where to start. Perhaps I shall work my way up from simple to complex, yes?"

Her Friend brightened, nodded. "If you are feeling like a skunk that day, I have an aesthetician I can recommend."

My hastier readers may be wondering: why does The Woman not simply fork herself groomed? Or perhaps: why does The Woman not get a massage or some similar form of touch that does not involve dragging a comb through fur?

The answer to this, at least from your humble narrator's limited point of view, is that there is loveliness in the touch, yes, but there is loveliness also in the way that one might ensure that another is well groomed. It is a way of coming closer. It is a way of sharing, and understanding that one is not alone. That is what I feel, at least, and I like that I can feel not alone at times, even if at other times I all but demand it.

And so it was that The Woman began simply, waiting until she was quite firmly a skunk before going to visit this contact Her Friend had given her.

The Aesthetician who greeted her at the door looked to be more than a hundred years old—more than a thousand!—and yet they moved with a sprightliness that surprised The Woman.

They all but pranced around her as they guided her to a comfortably padded table, something that could just as easily be molded down into a seat or some more complicated contraption.

"A skunk! An Odist!" they chirped. "You were sent by No Hesitation?"

The Woman tamped down the burgeoning sense of overstimulation and bowed. "Yes. End Of Endings of the Ode clade."

"Lovely lovely lovely. Please, please come in and lay down. I do so love grooming you and yours."

And so The Woman went inside and lay down and let The Aesthetician work through her mane and over her tail and through all the little nooks and crannies around her neck and limbs. All the while, they chatted quietly—for an aesthetician such as this reads their clients well and knew how to modulate their attitude that they not overwhelm someone such as The Woman. The brushing was calm and peaceful and felt lovely and delightful in all those ways that she appreciated when she was able to do it herself, and yet it came with a sense of companionship and camaraderie that left her feeling fulfilled and, yes, joyful. Joyful! The Woman and The Aesthetician talked and talked, and The Woman spoke more freely to her than ever she did to Her Therapist and, without being able to explain just how, she knew that the words she spoke would be kept in just as close a confidence.

The Woman left refreshed, renewed, reinvigorated, and with this eye she set to looking into the escalation that she promised Her Friend.

We have seen such success already, have we not? We have seen the ways in which The Woman—she who does not have many friends—enjoys the touch of hugs or a paw rested atop hers. It is a sometimes food, yes? But then, it is for all of us. I do not always want to be hugged or touched—I do not now, here on the edge of overflow—and there are forms of touch I do not like at all! The Woman here is considering intimacy, yes? Sensuality and sexuality? Those are things that I do not like. I like *that* they exist, I am glad that they do, and I even like writing about them—see, here! I am even about to do so!—but they are things that I hold at a distance from myself.

Ah, but my words are wandering. This touch, even the grooming, is a sometimes food for The Woman, and yet she had held herself at a distance from such for who knows what reason. I do not think she knew, herself, my friends, for she is as we all are: she is a woman who craves touch and deserves touch and does not, on an intellectual level, wish that she were *not* touched. It is emotional, perhaps, or psychic, or spiritual, or on some level other than the intellectual that the desire to touch and be touched, or the physical need for fulfillment, is difficult for her.

And thus The Woman began her slow climb up the ladder of escalation. She met once more with Her Friend and asked, kindly, perhaps a bit nervously, for a hug and for the chance to hold hands and paws—for she was a human that day, and Her Friend a skunk as ever—and it took something of a force of will to let such touch linger. It was a pleasant sensation and a pleasant conversation that followed, an exploration—between friends, for Her Friend was always careful to specifically *not* be The Woman's therapist—of meanings and boundaries.

And so it was that The Woman sought out those who she

knew, those who might have some affection for her beyond simple conversational friendship, those who had been sensual of old, partners and almost-partners from centuries ago who remained still on the System. She thought back through the years and years and years, and Her Lover was the one who leapt most readily to mind.

*"My dear, it has been some time since we have spoken,"* she sent over a sensorium message, *"for which I do apologize. Much of that is on me. I did wish to reconnect, though; would you be amenable to that?"*

The response was immediate. *"End Of Endings! Oh my god! You have no idea how happy I am to hear from you! I heard there were losses in your clade and was so worried I didn't even want to check if one of them was you."*

*"Not me, no. Should We Forget and No Longer Myself are no more, though."*

There was a long moment silence on the other end of the connection, though the sense of it lingering remained. *"I am sorry, love,"* Her Lover said at last. *"I haven't forgotten you, though, or my fondness, so yeah, I'd love to reconnect."*

If my more recently uploaded friends feel some sense of curiosity about how it is that someone with whom one has let contact languish for decades might still feel fondness after so long, or how one might not forget, you must remember that those who live sys-side remain functionally immortal. If one leans into such a fact, then decades spent away may as well be a blink of an eye, yes? If one leans into the everlasting memory with which we are blessed or cursed or which is simply bestowed upon us without further thought, then a past lover away from whom one has simply drifted amicably is just as easily recalled.

We are very old, you see. Why, at this point, I am 323 years old! And The Woman is of the same clade, so the same is naturally true of her—if she lives still, that is. To us, we remember being mortal as only some distant thing from so long ago. We have our identity as those who may live life slowly. Things may still come at us quickly, yes, but we can deal with them in parallel, can we not? I could get a note from my beloved up-tree stating that it is lonely or bored or simply hungry and wants someone to eat with, and so I may continue writing while joining em in this simple pleasure. I did that just earlier today, when she mentioned wanting to eat something good, some comforting food she learned from eir own friend, so that good memories may also be cherished. When I did join it for a simple meal of *ciorbă de praz* and *ardei umpluți*—for you see, its friend is Romanian and taught em so many of the dishes that she now loves—I sat and listened and remembered and talked and ate and perhaps also fretted over stepping away from work, but I allowed myself to take some slowness, too. Even I am allowed such things, yes? Even the terminally busy may let one self stay busy while the other comforts and is comforted by those they are close to.

Ah, dear readers, I am sorry that I cannot keep my thoughts from wandering and letting my pen trail after them like an eager puppy—yes, just like The Woman's rituals—and that such interrupts the story I am trying to tell!

All of this to say that The Woman and Her Lover spent some years together back in the first century of the System, back after secession but before she had fallen into her gentle stasis, before the goal of processing trauma was subsumed by the trauma itself. They had met—and you will not believe this, friends!—they had met at the very same cafe where The Woman and Her Friend met only days before. They had stumbled across each other in the most romantic way possible: by ordering the same coffees at the counter. They both asked for the same mocha with extra whipped cream, gave each other a strange look, and then fell into laughter.

As is the case with so many cladists—yes, perhaps especially us—they orbited around each other eccentrically, coming now closer together, drifting now further apart. There would be a chaotic few weeks or months or years when they would dance or walk the field or sit and drink mochas or cook for each other or share a bed, and then, with a fond exchange of kisses, they would part ways with a promise to see each other again soon, for their lives were long and the System was wide.

Unlike so many other cladists, however, The Woman is too much herself. She is too alive and she is full to overflowing, and she seemed ever to become more and more herself, to overflow in ways subtle and dramatic. For, you see, The Woman had simply been human—a furry, to be sure! She always maintained that identity—for decades after forking and had focused on that goal of processing, but as she had to expend more and more energy to keep her thoughts well-ordered, she started to lose control of her form and her rituals began to overwhelm the order in her life. Her Lover helped how she could, loved her when she was a skunk or a panther as much as when she was a human, would never stand in the way of her rituals, but the more control she spent, the more energy she was without; the more time she spent trying to remain a realistic amount of herself, the harder it was for her to take in love from the outside.

And so, over the years, The Woman and Her Lover swung close together less and less often and for shorter and shorter intervals, and when The Woman requested time away, time to herself, Her Lover would kiss her on the cheek and smile and promise to see her again soon, and the smiles were more often sad, but The Woman held onto that promise, setting it up on her dresser or perhaps a high shelf where she might observe its austere grace along with that of all of the other promises she had been given over the years, for her life was long and the System was wide, and always they came back together.

My gentle readers, I would love to tell you that they met up at that selfsame cafe, but while life is poetic, not every meter is so strict. No, instead, they met up on a train.

A train! There are many things on Lagrange, this shared dream in which we live, and many things which have been perfected all the way down to their imperfections. When you collect so many minds all in one place and tell them to live their best and to live it forever, why, they will perfect precisely the things they love most and, my friends, I am sure I do not need to tell you that some people *love* trains.

As was their wont in decades past, The Woman met Her Lover onboard rather than on the platform. It was their habit for Her Lover to step aboard the train one stop after The Woman did, and for them to both hunt for a seat—no matter how empty the train was; for even if it was totally empty, the *perfect* seat is of the utmost importance—and to meet in the aisle. You see, when your relationship has its beginning in a chance meeting, sometimes it feels nice to seek out those chance meetings again, yes?

What better way to do so than on so linear a structure as a train? It certainly reduces the possibilities of near misses!

Somewhere near the front of the train, they met, and here they felt that welcome surprise. The "chance meeting" may have been deliberately constructed, and yet it was not without a sense of newness. The Woman was a familiar panther that day and Her Lover a human as always, but The Woman, who had been so focused on her stasis until now, realized at once that she *had* changed over the years. Slowly, to be sure, and perhaps not in the ways that she wished, but she had changed. Today, she wore a silver-gray wrap of a shirt, all shot through with purple threads, and a gray-silver wrap of Thai fisherman's pants, all shot through with threads of blue. Her fur may have been the same black, short and glossy, and she may have lingered in suffering as the tenth stanza had in her own way, but she was hardly the type to fully languish, nor wear the same thing for years or decades at a time!

"Kitty," Her Lover said, leaning on old affections and wide smiles, "you look amazing. Every time I see you I'm always so surprised to see you looking so...so chic!"

The Woman, caught up in the infectious ebullience of the greeting, smiled and bowed, tail lashing about with delight. "Thank you, Farai. You are looking well."

And indeed she was! The Woman was pleased to see just how well. Her Lover, she knew, kept to warmer sims and hotter climes and these little jaunts onto this kindly juddering railway through the mountains were aberrations of a sort, so the fact that her outfit appeared to be a skirt and blouse in oranges and reds covered in part by some hastily acquired hoodie displaying the logo of a band The Woman *knew* no longer existed made sense. It made her ache in some intangible way to not see those smooth-skinned arms she had spent countless hours nestled within, brushing dull claws over or stroking soft fingertips along, her pale white skin in such stark contrast, signifiers of some more physical past.

Still, within her face was that vivacity that had originally drawn The Woman in. There lay warmth that put the colors of her clothing to shame. There lay the kindness and wit in equal measure. There lay the lips she had kissed and the cheeks she had dotted her nose against and the high forehead she had touched her own to while they had shared quiet laughter and quieter I-love-yous.

The Woman cried, and Her Lover guided her to a seat that she might do so without needing to stand, trying to balance herself against the kind juddering of the train.

When she could speak again, she said, "I have missed you, my dear. I am pleased that your patience holds as ever."

"Of course it does, End Of Endings," Her Lover said with eager kindness. "Our relationship is as it is, and I knew that going into it."

"Still, there have been times over the years that I wished I had contacted you, and did not."

"Why, do you think?"

"After Death Itself and I Do Not Know quit, at first, I was in pain, and then I was bitter, and then I was lonely and glad of it, and then I was too absorbed in being myself, and then..." The Woman shrugged and gestured around vaguely, not at anywhere specifically, but at a world now lessened by the loss of 23 billion souls.

"Yeah. And then," Her Lover said, letting that statement stand in for ineffable grief. We live sometimes in aposiopesis, do we not? Silence, for only a few seconds, and then, "Is that why you got in touch?"

She shook her head. "Well, yes, but also, I have had some thoughts about joy and how to find it. I experienced it for a week or so, but it faded. However, I experienced it almost on accident, yes? And I wanted to be deliberate."

"Oh!" Her Lover sighed, slouching back in her seat with a smile on her face that was very nearly a silly grin. Not quite, but very nearly. "It's been a *long* time since someone has said something that flattering to me."

The Woman preened—and we all know that is quite cute!—which earned her a kiss to the cheek in return. She marveled at how easy it was to fall back into such lovely habits and, yes, there was joy to be had, there, and to that she clung tightly. It seemed not the time for her to bring up the task of finding joy specifically in touch, in sensuality and sexuality, though she knew Her Lover felt that such were joys as well. It was a matter of enjoying *this* joy, first.

And enjoy she did! Friends, I have had precious few lovers in my life as I am now, but certainly none like this. I am not unhappy, of course; I like who and what I am and how I engage with the world. Still, if ever there were anything to make me jealous of particular friendship, it would be something like this. It would be the friendship that is particular to The Woman and Her Lover. There is touch that I like and touch that is distracting, but if I could hold the hand or paw of someone as tenderly as these two held hands and paws now, if I could share a moment of quiet conversation such as this, I would in a heartbeat. I am gripped by my own rituals and demands, though, and have not the strength to fight them.

So it was that The Woman and Her Lover rested their hand and paw with palms together, fingers only slightly curled, on The Woman's knee and spoke of joy.

"I'm a little surprised that you came to me for touch," Her Lover said, half-smile on her face. "Not in a bad way, not at all. You know me, I love that, but that wasn't something you ever sought out from me *this* directly."

The Woman shook her head. "I know, and it has taken me energy to even get to this point, but if there is pleasure to be had, and if pleasure is a part of joy, then I ought to look, yes? If joy is my goal?"

Her Lover laughed, voice musical. "I see you're still very much yourself, love. Never change~"

With that, she leaned over to give The Woman another kiss to the cheek, and then another, this time at the hinge of her jaw, and then another and another, a meteor-shower down The Woman's neck, and there was joy in this, too, and purring to be heard.

They laughed together at their touches and their brazenness and their shared joy. They shared their nuzzles and their giggles and they, as the poet says, shared their oranges and gave their kisses like waves exchanging foam.

My lovely readers, there is more that happened—and I am going to tell you! I really will, because it is important to the story, of course, and because it is important to our lives sys-side and to us as a clade and it was important to The Woman and Her Lover—but, dear ones, if you would like to skip ahead, to cover your eyes and curate your experience or to simply let them have their moment together, know that our lives sys-side and our clade are complicated and that The Woman and Her Lover were complicated, too, and so was the joy they found. Know that they also, as the poet says, shared their limes and gave their kisses like clouds exchanging foam.

They leaned on each other as they stepped lightly from the train to the platform, and, although the station was a loveliness in its own right, their conversation had spurred within them both a desire to explore and gladly, rather than their feet hitting the cement of the platform, they landed instead on the cool, hardwood floor of Her Lover's home where The Woman brushed her fingertips featherlight against the still-familiar jamb.

There was no rush to their movements, for both The Woman and Her Lover had always been methodical in their sensuality. Perhaps it fit the mold of one of The Woman's rituals—she must touch here, first, and then she would kiss there, and only then would she brush her fingers there, across the cheek—and perhaps not—a logical progression remains a logical progression without the hint of ritual.

There was no rush to their movements, and so they sat first on the couch, sharing their kisses, refamiliarizing themselves with each other. The Woman felt within a subtle twisting, a stirring, a clockwise motion that dragged with it two colors of emotions. There was the love rekindled, there, yes, and there was along with it a growing anxiety: there was something less than worry and more than thought. In the middle, there was a spot between joy and fear, a place of too much meaning that she could not pin down. Arousal, perhaps? For there was that, there, too. That was perhaps of that clockwise turning: the slow swell of warmth low in her belly and the gentle pressure within her chest and bristle of whiskers. Excitement, maybe? Anticipation?

Here was another thing for The Woman to set before herself where she might observe it, describe its shape by the way the orange and blue of love and anxiety swirled around it.

But, ah! Here, too, was Her Lover. Here was a soul she treasured. Here was a body she cherished. Here was this spot—just beneath the chin—which, when kissed, elicited a shiver, and this spot—at the hollow of the throat—which, when brushed with a fingerpad, elicited something both gasp and giggle. Here was arousal and excitement and anticipation in equal measure. Here was a thing for her to focus on that was not the cool blue of anxiety that warred with love remembered in unequal measure.

There was no rush to their movements, though, and arousal and excitement and anticipation in equal measure are a joy in their own, and so with some unspoken negotiation, The Woman leaned back and Her Lover leaned forward rather than the other way around. There was some careful tail maneuvering to accomplish this, but, my friends, we are used to it. There is *always* a careful maneuvering of our tails. Skunk tails, you must understand, are quite sizeable, and feline tails are less flexible at the base. It is a part of our lives, you see? There is still joy in having a tail, though, and with her tail out of the way, The Woman was once more able to relax, this time laid flat on her back, and Her Lover was once more able to provide that meteor shower of kisses down over the side of her neck, then over across her décolletage, and it was here where, as promised, the complications arose, for it was at that moment, at the moment where Her Lover's kisses landed upon that lovely spot at the hollow of her throat that there was a bright flash amidst the blue of The Woman's anxiety and she was no longer The Woman who was a panther, but instead The Woman who was human.

Both The Woman and Her Lover let out a startled exclamation and both froze where they were. The Woman froze because suddenly her clothes fit different and her field of view no longer included the bridge of a wide muzzle and her ears were positioned differently and there was no longer any fur mediating touch. Her Lover froze because...well, I do not rightly know, friends. We can guess, yes? We can guess that there was the shock of a new form, yes, but they knew each other well, did they not? We can guess that there was a shift on the couch beneath her with a different shape, different size, different weight of lover, but they knew each other well, did they not? They knew each other well, and so we may guess that Her Lover knew that such a shift was not always a pleasantness for The Woman, not always a joy.

"You okay, love?"

"I do not know."

"Want me to stop?"

The Woman squeezed her eyes shut and looked closer at the point of too much meaning described by love and by anxiety, found it still indescribable.

"End Of Endings?"

"No," she said at last. "No, I do not want you to stop. I will tell you if I do."

"Should I avoid that spot?"

"Kiss me there again."

Her Lover did so, to no effect, other than a quiet huff from The Woman. They looked at each other, then both smiled and shrugged in unison, their mutualism ever a loveliness between them.

And so they continued together with no rush to their movements.

The Woman shifted forms several times more. There were, they found, certain milestones that led to such, rather than certain places. There was the first hand on breast—and then she was a skunk. There was the first clutch of fingers at side—and then she was back to human. There was the feeling of warm fingers slipping beneath a waistband—and, yes, she was back to being a panther.

Throughout it all, all those kisses—whether or not The Woman was able to return them, for giving kisses with a muzzle is not a thing she was able to do—and those squeezes and strokes and the gentle way Her Lover cupped her palm over The Woman's mons, throughout all those shifts, The Woman kept before her that ineffable point. Throughout all of the warmth of love and those stinging-cold flashes of anxiety and they way they swirled clockwise, she peered closer that she might scry some meaning out of this kernel of what was most certainly not joy. Even as the warm wave of climax pushed through her, rushing out from that spot low in her belly, even as she clutched at Her Lover's shoulders, fingertips and clawtips both tugging at skin, even as her cries smoothed out into whine-tinged breaths, she tried to name the unnamable.

They lay together for hours after, talking and touching. They moved to the bed and The Woman who was a skunk or a human or a panther brought such pleasure as she had been given to Her Lover, and at last they slept, and the undefinable remained undefined. There was joy in that touch, in that remembered love, and she knew that Her Lover would be by her side for some time to come if she let her—and she would let her—and that, too, was a joy. And still, there between joy and fear...

There was joy, yes, but it was not a complete joy. Her hedonism with touch and sensuality and sexuality was a lovely hedonism and she cherished it, but it was not the hedonism she needed for this task.

Some of my readers may be wondering why it is that I know so much about The Woman.

"How does she know all of this?" some might be wondering. "Does she really know all these things that The Woman did? Does she know who the kindly shop owner is? The one who pet on The Woman as she sobbed from too spicy a chili?" Others might be wondering—and rightly so!—"How much of this is actually real? Surely she does not know The Woman's innermost thoughts! All this talk of ideas in shapes being set before her is quite silly."

My answer is that tired phrase: "It is complicated." Of course I do not know her innermost thoughts. I think it is a me thing to take abstract ideas and pretend they look like pretty baubles or hot coals or little statuettes to be placed upon a dresser. I cannot read minds, and I do not have any memories from The Woman. I do not even know quite what she is anymore! I would not know if she quit, since I am not down-tree from her—her down-tree instance is dead now, these last six decades, remember—and I do not believe she merged cross-tree with anyone except perhaps Ashes Denote That Fire Was, who is building in themself a gestalt of the clade as best they can. No, I do not know anything so intimate.

What I do have, though, is a story. I have the story I learned from The Woman's Friend and Therapist and Cocladist and Lover, the one I learned from The Blue Fairy. I have all of that story that I learned, and I have that story that I lived.

×

One day—I remember it being quite a warm one, though every sim has different weather, and we as a clade are not all that keen on cold—one day, The Woman came to me.

"Dear The Wheat And Rye Under The Stars," she said as she stood before my door, a skunk looking much the same as I do—though it bears repeating that she was *quite* stylish, and I promise you, friends, I am *not;* she wore a simple outfit of shifting colors that caught the eye without dazzling, one that made her look supremely comfortable as herself, and me? I wore a t-shirt and pajama pants! "I was pointed your way by Praiseworthy. Do you have a moment to speak?"

Readers, I do not think I need to tell you that I was caught off-guard by this! I had never met The Woman before, though I had certainly seen her once or twice. There were functions, yes? And perhaps she came to one of my readings or two, and certainly she was there, that day on the field as we watched Michelle who was also Sasha give herself up to the world and become one with the heart that perhaps beats at some imagined center of the System. The most recent time I had seen her, though, was in some unreadable and thus unwritable mood as some few dozen of us gathered on the first of what some are now calling *HaShichzur,* the day that Lagrange was restored after the Century Attack.

And now here she was, standing in the little courtyard created by the set of townhouses in which I and others within the ninth stanza live, with her paws clasped before her, bowing.

"Yes?" I said. I do not know why I asked it like a question, but that is what I did.

"I would like to ask you about your writing."

"Ah! Of course, my dear. Please, come in." I stood out of the way and gestured her inside, and this was the first time I saw her ritual of brushing her fingertips against the jamb of the door.

My place is clean and minimal. It is not clean because I am necessarily a clean person, nor is it minimal because I have any particular attachments to minimalism or its trappings. Friends, you have surely gathered by now that I am quite a bit more focused on writing than I am on most anything else. My home contains a simple kitchen and a simple dining table. There is a den in which there is a couch and a coffee table. There are two bedrooms, one of which contains a bed and the other of which is empty. The only room that is of any interest is perhaps my office, but even that is probably too minimal for most people's tastes! I have a desk. I have paper and pens and a keyboard on which I can type when that is the mood.

That is not to say that it is a boring place—at least, I do not think so! I have some paintings on the wall, some landscapes interrupted by hyper-black squares painted by The Child. There are several little decorations scattered around, as well: little objects that The Oneirotect has made in its explorations in oneirotecture and oneiro-impressionism. The most meaningful of these sits on my writing desk, and takes the form of a wire-frame polyhedral fox about the size of my paw. While it is silver in color, it does not cast any shadows on itself and has constant luminosity, and so it looks like a two-dimensional shape that changes as your perspective does.

Ah, I am digressing again. My thoughts and words wander.

The Woman came in, looked around, and smiled to me. It was a very kind smile, very earnest, and I have no other words but to say that I felt blessed by such a smile. "Your home is so comfortable. It does not feel at all overwhelming."

I nodded, feeling a wave of relief. "I am pleased you think so. Can I get you anything?"

"I would not say no to a glass of water."

While I fetched us both such a glass, I said, "What is it that brings you here? I hope that Praiseworthy had nice things to say about me."

"Quite nice, yes, though I find her a very curious skunk. She is elusive, perhaps? Not in that she is hard to find, but it is hard to pin down her mood or her thoughts."

"Oh, very much so. I remember being her, yes, but that was nigh on three centuries ago, and I do not quite understand who she has become, myself." I handed over the glass of water and gestured toward the couch, where we sat on either end, half-facing each other.

"She was still pleasant to be around, at least," The Woman said. "She said that I should seek you out, along with Where It Watches The Slow Hours Progress and Beholden To The Heat Of The Lamps. You are the last on my list."

"That is curious. What was the reasoning for those names?"

"A writer, a poet, and a musician. I have been having some thoughts on joy that I would like to explore with each of you."

She told me her story, much as I have written it to you, readers. She spoke of the ways of seeking out joy, of diving into the pleasures of food—and I can tell you, friends, she is absolutely correct about tam mak hoong; it is *incredibly* delicious—and the pleasures of touch and sensuality and sexuality. She told me of how much joy she had found in such things and in the rekindled relationship with Her Lover, and she also told me of how these joys were lovely, but not the joys that she was seeking, and that she had three more items on her list of five. She had entertainment, creativity, and shaping herself yet to go.

"So, your goal with visiting is to read?"

She shook her head. "I have already read. That is why I was sent to visit Slow Hours. She is a very quiet person, and very comfortable to be around, as you are. You are inexact mirrors of each other, are you not? She reads and you write. She loves poetry most while you love prose. She is human and you are a skunk. She is a bit frumpy and tousled, and you are quite neat and put-together."

I will admit, friends, that I looked down at my pajama pants and t-shirt and laughed. "I do not feel put together."

"Perhaps one never does," she said, "and yet you exist so well contained. The whole of you exists within the person sitting before me. You are Rye, the author. You are Rye, the sincere. You are Rye who is kind. You are these things and you are none other."

My readers will know well that I have too many words in me. Why, just look at all that I have written already! I have gone on

at length about Laotian food and lovers and friends and family and mochas and melancholy. I have accused myself already
a handful of times of intruding on my own story, of being helpless before the graphomania that guides my paw. So it is that
you must believe me when I say that I was left speechless. All of
this ceaseless torrent of words within me simply stopped.

I do not know if you have ever been complimented in just
the right way by just the right person, but if you have, you well
know that it is startling in its intensity. Had someone else said
these things about me, even my beloved up-tree, I might well
have blushed and stammered a thank you and felt good for the
rest of the day.

The Woman, this skunk who sat before me with a glass of
water held in her paws and her very chic outfit, the one who
had smiled to me with such earnestness as to be a blessing, this
woman who was too much herself, had just perceived me with
such force as to leave me feeling bowled over. Even today, even
these many years later, I remember that compliment and find
breath catching in my throat, and we have already spoken on
that, have we not?

We sat in silence, then, while I processed this. My friends,
you may perhaps have picked up the sense that The Woman is
in some fundamental way broken and perhaps unable to interact well with others. After all, she sits for so long in her room
and in her home and on her field, and she sees Her Friend only
with some small frequency, and had only just recently gotten in
touch with Her Lover, yes? And that is in many ways true, that
she is broken. But it is not *wholly* true. She was too much herself, yes, and she would have said even then that she had lived

for too long and that she would probably say that she was in some fundamental way broken, but she was also so much more! I have shown you all that she was through her own perception, but from the outside...ah, she was hard not to love, my friends.

"Thank you, my dear," I said at last, bowing.

She smiled—another blessing!—and nodded to me.

"Tell me about your reading, then."

"I visited Slow Hours in her library," she began. "I know that it belongs to the whole of Au Lieu Du Rêve, but she has inhabited it quite thoroughly, has she not?"

"She has, at that," I said.

"We sat in the solarium and spoke about what reading *is*. She spoke of taking a story or a poem and wrapping oneself up in it. She gave me an example. She recited a poem:

> "Too many suits move in too many lines.
> They circle banquet tables, hawk-eyed,
> hunting crudites, canapés, bruschetta.
> Fingers ferry food—fish, perhaps—finding
> slack-jawed mouths already open,
> squawking at wayward children
> or bemoaning The Market,
> whatever that may be.
>
> "At some point, who cares how long ago,
> death surfaced, claimed one, submerged again.
> Who knows how well they knew him,
> their backs turned, studiously
> deciding that he is no longer of them?

"One could never guess.

"We can say his suit was very fine, perhaps,
that the room is tastefully furnished,
the casket silver, the bar, open,
quite good, and none of them are drunk yet,
or at least none look it.

""Good man, good man," they mutter,
doing all they can to convince each other
through well-rehearsed performances,
that this must be the case.

"The silently bereaved already sit graveside."

I turned those words over and over in my head for a minute, since The Woman had seemed quite comfortable sitting in silence with me. She used that time to drink her water while I played back the words again and again, looking down at my paws, and then returned my gaze to hers. "There is a difference between the mere performance of grief and grieving itself, is there not?"

"It is as you say. There is performed grief and performative grief—performative in the philosophical sense. We of the tenth stanza were quite sad when Lagrange came back with us intact but not with Should We Forget. We received condolences from many, some flowers and many kind words. Ever Dream came over and spoke with me about grief as we sat out on the field, where she said, "It is quite sad, is it not? To lose someone you have known for so long is quite sad." I agreed, and then drew a line around the topic." She performed such a motion now, describing an arc before her with one of her well kept claws, before dismissing it with a wave. "This was grief performed."

I nodded, and in my heart, I think I knew what was coming next, for I found my muscles bunching up as in in preparation for something—flight, perhaps? I do not know, my friends.

"And Warmth In Fire came over, too, so that it could sit at our table and weep rather than eat. Ey wept, and then asked to retreat, and we guided her up to Should We Forget's room so that they could lay in her bed for a while in silence. When it came back downstairs, ey thanked us kindly and left, and when we went back upstairs to look, there was a flower wrought out of some subtly glowing metal left on Should We Forget's pillow. It lays there still."

"I remember that day," I said. "I will admit that I only met Should We Forget a handful of times, and always mediated through Warmth, so I do not have the context for that grief, other than the fact that ey was left in pain for some time after the restoration."

"That was performative grief," The Woman said. "That was grief that, through its expression, was made real. Warmth In Fire's grieving allowed us to grieve as well. Ever Dream and all of those who sent us flowers performed a grief that was only intellectual. I appreciate them for that, but I love Warmth In Fire for what ey gave us."

We as a clade cry easily, and it is a thing that we all like about ourselves. I like the fact that I can cry! I like that I can cry over my own writing, go back and read a scene I wrote wherein a character experiences too many feelings or some form of growth and cry along with them.

So it is perhaps no surprise that I cried then, and that, for the third time, The Woman sat with me in silence.

When I was once more able to speak, after I had taken a moment to clean up, I asked, "You went into this experience with Slow Hours to explore joy, yes? What did you find, in the end?"

"I did not read only this one poem. I read several more with her that day, and took home several books to read in such a way. Slow Hours talked me through the joy of stories—even the small ones—and left me with some assignments.

"I did not like all of the books, but Slow Hours instructed me to read them anyway, unless they started to make me truly bored. None did, however, so I finished every book I took with me.

"Of the five books I brought home, one made me quite upset for how viscerally uncaring the protagonist was. I found them acting for reasons that I did not understand, as though they were a being solely of habits and not of thoughts or emotions. One made me cry for the way the protagonist was torn down and yet built herself into someone new. The other three books I found quite enjoyable, and they were all engrossing to greater or lesser extent.

"I found this form of reading to be fulfilling, yes, but also all-encompassing. When I read in the manner that Slow Hours suggests, by wrapping myself up in the story and letting it play out in my head, I found that I became more easily engrossed, yes, but also I found myself wrung out at the end of each. I would finish a book and then have to lay in bed for ten hours straight, sleeping off and on. When I brought this up with Slow Hours, she only smiled, shrugged, and said that appreciation takes as much energy as creation.

"There *was* joy there, though. It had been many, many years since I had read something so thoroughly, had so completely taken it within myself. It was nothing so trite as feeling as though I was living there with the characters, nor that I was unable to put the book down. It was a relishing. It was a savoring. Each word became a part of my world, drifting into view to be cherished and then back out of it. By the third book, I saw what it was that Slow Hours meant by wrapping oneself up in a story, and I found comfort in this."

I stayed silent as I listened. After all, to hear so intriguing a person speak so eloquently on the act of reading was lovely! I never learned whether any of the five books that she read thus were mine, and I was too afraid to ask. I do not know why, friends, but I was feeling quite outclassed. The Woman had a quiet force to her personality that I cannot deny, and I wonder to this day whether she knew this about herself.

"You do not seem too pleased with this as an outcome," I said.

She shrugged. "It was a step on a path. I also sought out entertainment in other forms. I spoke next with Beholden, who provided me a similar approach to listening to music. We spoke about active listening and what it means to actually hear a song, to, yes, wrap oneself up in it. We spoke about songs and albums, movements and pieces, and the stories that each of them can tell. Did you know that our dear Beholden has recently completed a concept album about the Century Attack? I did not listen to this for her assignments, per her request, but I did after the fact.

"I ran into a similar sensation, however. I *did* find joy in this type of listening, as I prowled through–" At this, the woman's form rolled over in a wave and, with a quiet sigh, she was no longer a skunk, but instead a panther, black and with shining fur. She readjusted her clothing and continued. "As I prowled through the music that Beholden suggested, I found a depth to the act that I had never before experienced. I was able to wrap myself up in sound and lose myself within it. Even with the music that I did not particularly like, I was able to find appreciation and tease out organization.

"Beholden's concept album, when I listened to it thus, left me in tears." She laughed quietly, and I felt comforted that I was present to hear such. "This is perhaps obvious, yes? A concept album surrounding the Century Attack, where we lost so many of our very own?

"There were no lyrics to this album, though, so it was not the words that made me cry. I was not listening to words, but I *was* listening to voices. I was listening to the voices of her up-tree, Beholden To The Music Of The Spheres, and her partner's up tree, A Finger Curled. She had delved into her sample library and pulled together all of the clips that she had recorded of those two and built about an hour's worth of music out of them. A Finger Curled, who was lost in the Attack, and Beholden To The Music Of The Spheres, who quit out of despair one week later. It was her threnody. It was her wailing song."

Readers, I am not ashamed to say that I cried again. How could I not, after all? I had met Beckoning and Muse, before, myself. They had invited me over some few years before the Century Attack to let me research their gardens. They had fed me a dinner of pasta with zucchini, and a desert of zucchini bread, for their harvest was too large by far. We had sat out on the deck and looked out over the grass and the little raised beds that Beckoning had tended for a century or more and, although my paws itched to return home to write, we spoke until long after the sunset on our joys and sorrows, our hopes and fears.

I cried, and through it all, The Woman sat in kind silence.

When, now for the second time, I was able to sit up straight again, able breath slowly, able to look at The Woman instead of my paws as I covered my face, I bowed to her and said, "Thank you for telling me these things. I did not realize just how much I needed to hear them."

"Why?"

The Woman's simple question left me all the room in the world to admit that I did not know. I think that until she asked it, I was not quite sure why, myself. I *had* needed to hear those things but, yes: why? I do not think I would have been able to tell her as part of my statement, but that syllable forced my thoughts into order in a way that they are not as I write this, six years later.

"Because I have not internalized the immediacy of the attack," I said. "I did not know Should We Forget. I never met No Longer Myself. I met and spoke with Beckoning and Muse, yes, but only once. You telling me these things—me hearing them— was enough to make me realize that I have not truly grieved them, not properly. Your story of Warmth grieving helped me understand em better, and your story of Beholden's music and how she told you not to listen to it for her assignments made me realize that I, too, am only just starting to process the loss."

"I understand. I was forced to confront the immediacy of Should We Forget no longer being with us from the very first day, and I am used to thinking of my stanza in terms of loss. We lost Death Itself and I Do Not Know, yes? We knew loss in a way more immediate within the clade except perhaps by those of the second stanza, who lost their first line, too, yes?"

"Was there a difference for you? Death Itself and I Do Not Know quit, but Should We Forget was taken from you."

The Woman tilted her head, then gazed out the sliding glass door that led out to my little patio. "I think I knew, on some level, that Death Itself would leave us. I certainly suspected when she went all but catatonic, yes? But I knew. I had no such foreknowledge of Should We Forget leaving us. I suspect that none did, except perhaps Slow Hours, and she told me that her dreams did not make sense until after the fact." She returned her gaze to me. "So yes. There was a difference. The feelings surrounding Death Itself and I Do Not Know are a tired acceptance. They *were* a tired acceptance even immediately after. The feeling surrounding Should We Forget is a sharp and cold grief. It is a feeling of my world being upended and my footing no longer being sure."

"It did not feel stable after Lagrange came back, no."

"It did not. That, I am told, is why Beholden wrote her threnody: Beckoning was lost to the Attack and Muse quit out of grief one week later. Beholden, fearing that her life was unstable, declined the merge. She told me that she feared that accepting it would change who she was on a fundamental level, only for her to die, not loving her partner in the same way that she had for hundreds of years beforehand. A Finger Pointing has

Beckoning's memories from regular merges, but Muse is truly dead, now. Her memories have been dismissed and cannot be retrieved."

"I see," I said. "And so she memorialized what memories she did have in the form of her samples."

"There are many memorials now, are there not? There are many tokens. There are many metallic flowers and songs of laughter."

I smiled. "There is poetry in your words, my dear."

She bowed from where she sat, smiling. "And so I come to you, Rye."

"So you do. You have read with Slow Hours. What shall we do to help you on your path to joy?"

"Write."

I laughed. I do not think it was an unkind laugh, but it was a startled one. I am a writer, yes, but I do not fancy myself much of a teacher. I run regular workshops, yes, and offer what help I may, but I am first and foremost a writer. I do not think I am much of a collaborator, either. I get quite protective of my work, and I can be something of a bitch when it comes to having it challenged. "How shall we write, then?" I asked. "I write with A Finger Pointing. We send each other letters back and forth, telling stories."

"Perhaps that is a thing we can do, too, but this is a project that I would like to approach as a conversation. I do not have an agenda for how, simply that I must."

"Have you written before?"

She shook her head. "No, I have not. I have not created much since becoming who I am, I am sorry to say. My stanza will occasionally tell each other stories, however, and I always fancied myself quite good at that."

I nodded. "A story is a good place to start, yes. You really have made so little?"

"My last century has been spent focusing inwards and meting my time out carefully for reasons I cannot explain. I have been seeking a form of stillness, perhaps."

Ah! This was it! My friends, this was the point when I realized just what it was that made each of The Woman's smiles feel like blessings and what made it feel like she bore some power within her that I could not quite understand. It was her *stillness.* My astute readers will remember that she had a thought, some few thousand words ago: perhaps this unbecoming that her mind circled around was simply the utmost in stillness.

Now, your narrator did not know this at the time—I do not even know now that this was the thought she had that day, but I am a storyteller, and so that is part of her story—but at the time, it was a revelation. Stillness and stillness and stillness. What a dream to have! Would that I could find such, yes? Even now, even as I write this, I feel that the lucidity in my words here is due only to my recounting of a conversation I actually had, words anchored to moments in time that I pull out one right after the other and lay in a pretty row.

At the time, however, I said, "Have you found stillness in your endeavors so far? Was there stillness in active reading and active listening?"

"Not at all, no. I do not speak of physical stillness, but stillness of spirit. I shift forms, yes? I came to you as a skunk, yes? That is a physical restlessness that is evidence of an inner restlessness. My thoughts are unsettled. My feelings are unsettled. My mind is turbulent."

"That being the reason you did not feel the joy that you wanted?"

She nodded. "Yes. My thoughts became ordered, perhaps. That turbulence became a purposeful movement; rather than a stormy ocean, they were a river."

"I am sorry to say that I do not think my books would be any different."

"Oh, they are not," she said, chuckling. "They are quite good, of course, but they are hardly meditative."

I laughed as well. "Thank you, I think. I have a few that are labeled 'meditations on whatever', but even those probably do not fit the bill."

"I would assume not. No, I came to you because I wanted to talk to you specifically about creating not just on Praiseworthy's suggestion, but also because I watched And We Are The Motes In The Stage-Lights paint while visiting Beholden."

"Ah! Motes! What a delight!"

"She is, yes, though she is also quite a lot, is she not?"

I laughed, nodding.

"I will admit that, although I would agree that she is a delight, she was perhaps too much for me. When I first arrived at my visit to the house on the hill, she had just been swimming and was running around here and there."

"How old was she that day?"

"She said that she was seven," The Woman said. "I found her joy to be quite different from what I imagine for myself, though, as ought to be the case for someone who has chosen to live as a seven year old versus someone who has perhaps no choice but to live as a 317 year old, yes?"

"I will say that she is no less flighty or energetic when she chooses to live at older ages. When she is, say, twenty five, there is still no stopping her."

"So I am told. However, she is also a very good girl, is she not? Beholden saw the state that I was in—for when Motes started zipping around the house, I started shifting between forms—and suggested that she go and paint. She said quite simply"Okay!" and ran off to the next room where she sat on a stool and began painting."

I looked up to the wall beside the couch, upon which a painting sat. The Woman smiled and nodded.

The painting was of my up-tree's house. The Instance Artist was one who decided that it had had quite enough of life in comfort, life here on Lagrange, life here honing, or perhaps forging new frontiers but in a familiar place, and up and left for the stars, back when humanity buckled down and decided to send out the two launch vehicles. Our very own twins, yes? Castor and Pollux? Those two half-sized Systems that even still race out of the Solar System at some unimaginable speed, yes? The Instance Artist left us all behind with no fork to spare, and broke all of our hearts.

When it had lived here on Lagrange, though, it had contracted my other up-tree, The Sim Designer, Serene; Sustained And Sustaining, to build for it an infinite short-grass prairie. It was a land of long, rolling hills and yet longer flat basins that always drank most thirstily from the seasonal storms that did their best to thrash the Earth below. There, amid the countless acres, sat its house, low and flat, an echo of the plains around it all done up in concrete that matched so well the gray-tan stalks of the grass in fall, the gray-green stalks in spring, and glass.

And so there on my wall sat a painting that I had asked The Child to make, small by her standards at only the size of both of my paws held flat, wherein she had painted the house, the endless prairie, and the sky that somehow managed to be something beyond endless. There was the gray of the concrete that matched so well the gray-tan stalks of grass in fall, the gray-green stalks in spring, and glass. There was the plain, the sky.

And there, right in the center, hovering a scant claw-width above the house, a perfectly black perfect square.

Readers, you must understand that, when I say perfectly black, I do mean it! There is this color—or non-color—*Eigengrau* that is perhaps the darkest you are used to seeing. If you are in a perfectly dark room, or you are out beneath the stars at night and you close your eyes, or you are hiding under two layers of blankets from the monsters that haunt us still, even in this afterlife that we have built up into our nigh-perfection, what you see is not pure black, but *Eigengrau*. It is the darkest color, I am told, that our eyes can see, phys-side! This is because, even when there is no light, the nerves of our eyes still fire occasionally. Perhaps it is because this is something that is required for nerve cells to feel healthy, and when those cells are in our muscles and it is just one or two at a time, it does not yank our hand away from our pen and paper like they were burning hot, but when they are in our eyes, every little firing is still perceived as a photon hitting this rod or that cone. Perhaps it is because there is some fundamental state of being for us that is *not* stillness, but that is movement at some molecular level. Perhaps it is simply because they are lonely! I do not know, I do not know. I do not know.

This square is not *Eigengrau*. It is beyond that. It is beyond even black! It is an impossible black. It is deeper than *Eigengrau*, yes, but it is also a very thirsty black. If the ground of The Instance Artist's prairie drinks thirstily of the sky, so too does this black drink thirstily of all the light in the world. It draws light from the room, and when you look at the painting, the world seems dimmer. It is a hole in the world.

I am used to it, my friends, for it sits happily enough upon my wall, but I am told by some that it is unnerving to see.

"Her paintings have always struck me as bearing a sort of serenity that I have not actually seen in the world," I said after we had appreciated house and plain and sky and hole in the world. "It is more than just some moment of movement captured and frozen in time. It is like she records things that had never been anything but still to begin with."

"Yes, and that is what drew me to her," The Woman said, gaze lingering on the painting. "I begged Beholden's leave to sit and watch Motes for nearly an hour. I claimed a spot in her studio once I received permission and watched as she worked. While I was there, she built up a scene of a mesa. I recognized it as Table Mountain. Do you remember?"

"Yes," I said, with some surprise. "I have not thought of that place in...well, likely not since we uploaded!"

She laughed. "Neither had I. We hiked there once and it seems to have left little enough impression, and Motes simply pulled it up from some deep recess, yes? Seeing that slowly take shape, though, as she worked with her paints, I felt like I was seeing some ancient behemoth who had never once woken laying asleep. It was a mountain that had never moved and never changed, even as a suburb sprawled at its base."

"Did she paint the shape while you were there?" I said, gesturing to the black-beyond-black square.

"No, not while I was looking. I did still have my errand, yes? I did not want to lose track of that. I wish now that I had."

"Having watched her paint this one, I can tell you that it is both more and less important than the rest of the painting. She paints it much as she paints the rest of the painting, yes? She brings one foot up onto her stool so that she can rest her chin on it and her tail drapes down behind her and she listens to her very strange music, and she paints the rectangle. Perhaps she sticks her tongue tip out as she does so, like she is concentrating very hard, yes?" I stuck my tongue tip out just so, furrowing my brow and squinting as though at some minute detail.

The woman laughed.

"So it is much like she paints the rest of the scene, yes? Except that it is not, because she is not adding to the picture, she is taking away from it. I have tried to look at this painting from every angle, yes? I have looked up close and far away. I have touched it and smelled it and—yes, I will admit—tasted it, and it is in all ways just paint on canvas. But it is not on *top* of *anything,* it is *through everything,* I would say. I do not know how else to explain it. With all the calmness in the universe, she excised a part of the world from existence." I looked up to the painting again. "I feel that, were I able to visit Dear's prairie again, that very chunk of it would be missing. I fear it would be some sort of black hole hungrily gobbling up all of Lagrange from the inside. In my dreams, that is what the Century Attack looks like. In my dreams, we are all pulled through a null rectangle like that, and when the world is pulled back out, those like Should We Forget and No Longer Myself and Beckoning and Muse are left within."

We sat in silence—silences can be so comfortable sometimes!—while I looked up at the painting and The Woman looked out the sliding glass door that led out to my little patio. It must have been two or three minutes of just long, comfortable silence, of just a woman who was also a cat and a woman who was also a skunk, two women who were in some roundabout way the same, sitting together.

"How large do you suppose it would be?" The Woman said, startling me out of my reverie.

"Mm? The rectangle? The hole?"

She nodded.

"I go back and forth. Sometimes, I feel that it is right in front of me and the house is in the distance, and that it is painted to scale so that it is quite small. Sometimes, I feel like it must be behind the house, or way out beyond the sky, and it is larger than the moon."

"I see we understand it in the same way. I cannot tell, either. I can tell you, though, that watching Motes brought me the closest to the joy that I have been seeking than I have ever been." She frowned down to her glass, now empty. When she continued, her speech was halting, slow, thoughtful. "Not...for me, not my own joy, and I think not even for her, though the little skunk certainly seems quite joyful. It is...adjacent to the joy. It brought me near to the joy, but did not necessarily bring the joy to me."

×

We talked for some time more, The Woman and I, and discussed what it was that we could do to help her find joy. I am sorry to say, though, that we were not able to come up with something.

We circled for some time around meditative acts and how that might work with writing. Automatic writing, perhaps? Should The Woman set up with a note book and a pen and look into some deeper self and begin to write? Should she bid my demon of graphomania visit her, grab her by the wrist, drag her pen across the page that words may flow after it like eager puppies?

No, no. That was not it.

Should she journal? Should she write what she felt during the day? Should she boil the ceaseless moments of her life down to vignettes? Should she make those around her into caricatures that only showed those bits worthy of being set to paper?

No, no. That was not it, either.

Friends, I will note that, even though I got a little bit frustrated with myself, these *were* good discussions. I was frustrated with myself because I wanted to help in this endeavor. It was a good idea! It was a good task. I wanted to help but I was not able to succeed, not that day.

So it was that The Woman returned home with the promise to come back the next day after we had both slept on it.

"For whom do you write, Rye?"

I had an answer ready for this, dear readers, for this is something that I think about with some frequency. "I write for those who need to read."

The Woman tilted her head—she was back to being a skunk, yes, but this is a habit that all of us share within the Ode clade, no matter our shape. "I have heard it said so often that one should write for oneself and wait for an audience to come."

"That is popular advice, is it not? There is joy in writing things that no one will read, I will not lie, but that is not how communication works. I would prefer instead to say,"Write what you want to see others reading." I would say, "Write what you believe others should know." To write solely for yourself is for the act of journalling, not for the act of creation."

She furrowed her brow. "I will admit that I spent last night thinking much on this. I thought of our conversation and the types of things that I might write and was stuck on the fact that what joy I am seeking is unrelated simply to an act but more to a way of being. Why, after all, would I simply put pen to paper and then close the book? That is just the motions of writing without a goal." A faint smile tugged at the corner of her mouth and, yes, this, too, was a blessing. "Though I am told that there is joy in fine pens and fine paper, too."

I laughed, reached into a pocket, and withdrew my current favorite pen. It is, you may be surprised to hear, quite plain. It is round and it is long. It has a cap that posts on the back. The nib is nothing special. It is a demonstrator—that is, it has a clear body so that one can see the ink within—but so are many of my pens. No, there is little special about it overall, other than the fact that it simply fits well within my paw, and that, dear friends, is what is most important in a pen.

I handed the pen over to The Woman and she drew a notepad

out of the air, wrote a few short sentences on it with the pen, nodded appreciatively, and handed it back. "It is a joy to write with, my dear. But to my point, I suspect there is goodness in the act of writing, but not the fulfillment I am seeking."

I nodded. "I would agree with that, yes. You speak of a way of being. You speak of not just creating, but of being a creative."

"Just so."

We sat in silence for a minute or so, simply enjoying our mochas—readers, by now you must know that we are nothing if not ourselves—while we each considered the direction of our conversation. It is not comfortable for me to be unable to address a thing that I feel I ought to be able to. When presented with a problem that even sounds like it *might* be within my bailiwick, if I cannot, it is in some key way dysphoric to me. The best I can manage, as I did then, was to recast the problem into a conversation. It does not remove the dysphoria, for I still have not solved anything, but it has set it aside, perhaps just in the other room. There is a selfishness in me.

At last, I said, "Would it be alright if I were to invite over Warmth? It is my beloved up-tree, of course, but ey also has thoughts on this that may help us find inroads to your fulfillment."

The Woman smiled and nodded. "By all means, please do."

We are the most of us not tall women, just as Michelle who was Sasha was not tall: just a little over a meter and a half or, as our literature professor described her in class after she read some saccharine ode by John Keats, "Miss Michelle Hadje, five foot four."

That '*most*' that I have written just now is doing much work, however. Several of us are taller. Why, I remain just an few centimeters taller than Michelle who was Sasha stood, but I might just as easily be mistaken for her when she appeared as a skunk, so similar are we. Oh! And The Oneirotect's sometimes-partner, Hold My Name Beneath Your Tongue And Know, towers over me by a head.

Several of us are shorter. The Child, as you will see, is understandably shorter. My little readers who sit cross-legged on carpet squares, perhaps you can picture her, for she is precisely as I have named her: a child.

The Oneirotect, my beloved up-tree, is not quite a child, and yet she is small. I think she is small enough that some would perhaps confuse her for one in the same way that The Child is a child, and I think that this may indeed be a little bit of transgression in which ey revels. She is tiny, perhaps even smaller than The Child, perhaps just over one meter high!

It also has within it a level of energy that may well contribute to this childlike nature. It zips and zooms and careens off walls as easily as does The Child—easier, perhaps, for even if she is only a few centimeters shorter, she is far more slender, far more lithe, borderline wiry, and she embodies the jitteriness that one might assume were I to call it 'critter'.

But no, ey is not a child. The Child owns that identity for herself. She leaned into the youngest sister of the fifth stanza, she owned *youngest* as meaning childhood, as was her choice. The Oneirotect, however, is simply the most recently claimed line, and is thus the youngest of all Odists with a snippet of our superlative friend's words to call its own. Ey lack the being-a-kidness and dwell instead in eir own transgressiveness: their fur is mussed and seemingly perpetually stained with the colors of grass and dandelions, her personality is as untameable as the unruly mane atop her head, and its care is as boundless as its emotions.

They are *all* of our youngest sibling and she is my beloved up-tree.

*"Warmth, my dear, would you be able to spare a fork to join me for a conversation with End Of Endings?"* I asked via a sensorium message.

*"Oh!"* came the immediate reply. *"Oh, of course! I have not spoken with her in too long. Right now?"*

*"If you have the bandwidth, yes."*

Rather than reply to my message directly, ey simply blinked into being in the entryway of my little townhouse. Had I some other guest over, perhaps it would have skitter-scattered and bounced around as it at times did, but you will remember, dear readers, that The Oneirotect was well-acquainted with the tenth stanza, and knew well that they dwelt comfortably in calm and quiet, and so she simply stepped lightly toward us, forking as ey went to pad up to both of us and give us each a hug. I leaned down to give a kiss between the skunklet's ears, ruffled up its already quite tousled mane, and smiled as she quit.

"Hi, End Of Endings," they said, smiling up to The Woman.

Once she had straightened up after returning the hug, The Woman smiled back down to them. "Warmth In Fire, it is lovely to see you, as always. How are you keeping, these days?"

"As best I can," ey said, tugging at the seat of a chair, raising it up, pulling and shaping until ey had a stool on which to sit, joining us around the table where we sat with our drinks, our water and our mochas. "I was not expecting to get a message to come over and see you, though. How are you?"

The Woman shrugged, the barest hint of her shoulders to go with an expression that bordered on unconcerned, as though the question were a valid one, but perhaps not worth answering. It was a very Talmudic shrug, you see, and, my friends, whenever one or the other of us pulls that off well, we feel *quite* proud. "My days are my days and my nights are my nights. I have things I wished to talk with you about, but beyond that, my life is simply my life."

The Oneirotect nodded. "Okay. I am glad to hear that you are still living your life," she said with a grin, a brief, rhythmic sway of her tail providing accompaniment for the mood. "What is it you wanted to talk about?"

The Woman looked to me, so I took up the lead. I asked my beloved up-tree, "Perhaps you could speak to what it is that you actually do my dear. What is it that you enjoy? We have been talking about such things."

"Well, I think of myself most of all as an aficionado of association, an oneirotect—a construct artist, if you must be such a bore," it answered. "One must bring into being a careful synthesis of memories both sensory and emotive, yes? For that is the substance of significance, yes?"

The Woman tilted her head in that way so familiar to us. "Nostalgia, then?"

"Yes!"

"Is there a draw to that for you? Or is that something you find others hungering for?"

The Oneirotect, clearly delighted by so simple a question,

brought its paws together over the table, folded neat and prim. "Yes, and also yes!" It let the humor of that comment stew for a moment before offering something more worthy of the title 'answer'. "In the first decades of the System, it was necessary to create the stuff that makes up our consensual dream, yes? We desired to eat, but none had yet dreamt of food; we wished to surround ourselves with cherished things, but even the platonic form of such did not yet exist.

"I find joy in creating these constructs—these *things*, this *stuff*, all that we interact with here—but most of all I enjoy the research that goes into that."

"I see," The Woman said. "So you worked on early foods, then? On staples, or on more beloved things?"

"I see you have done your own research, my dear." It offered a little bow, beaming up at The Woman. "That, or Rye spilled the beans."

I chuckled, shrugged.

"Very well. I favor culinary constructs now, but that has only become the case since I met Codrin. That said, I did begin with fruits we never got to try growing up in the Central Corridor. Most of the heavy lifting with staples had already been done by the time I began exploring oneirotecture, but there remained gaps in what was available. That experience was most formative, but it was Codrin's cooking that sent me down this path."

"Not ██████████? Not Codrin and Dear's partner?" The Woman asked. She asked, of course, after one remembered fondly, and one whose name is not yours to know, dear readers, or perhaps you know it intimately, but with a wink and a nudge like a joke kept between us. "Are they not the chef?"

The Oneirotect smiled wryly. "Well, sure, but my interest lies more in the food that others love to their core. ████████'s food is delightful, yes. It is *enjoyable,* and often it is *loved,* but it is not really *beloved.* I would rather focus on the food those remember with fondness their mothers and grandmothers cooking. Remembered foods. Cherished foods, yes?"

"I suppose this is where the nostalgia comes in, then, yes? Reaching back for the things that others loved, rather than simply ate out of necessity?"

The Oneirotect tilted its head, unruly mane falling over its eyes. Out of instinct, I reached over to brush it back into some semblance of order and got a rather wet lick to my wrist for my trouble. My friends, my beloved up-tree is quite weird.

"It is not as if none before me had dreamt of food just like grandma used to make, but what I offered was particularly attuned to that, yes."

"You speak of research and gaps in selections and beloved meals," I said. "It sounds like you speak most of all of making things for others, or for all, rather than for yourself."

"For others, I would say. That bit of communalism implied by 'all' did not come until much later. No, instead I drummed up interested parties from the feeds. These were the days that reputation and the markets had more meaning, yes? I still needed the rep for my work, for research into foods unfamiliar to me." They smiled wryly. "I was not without, of course, for I had been dipping my toes into instance artistry beforehand, before Dear forked, yes? But still, I needed the reputation for research, and I needed the research for commissions others asked of me."

There was a moment of silence as The Woman parsed this,

her gaze distant. When her focus returned, she said, " 'Before Dear forked'? Am I to infer that this is when you were Rye? Or am I missing something in the cladistics?"

"I am not the first to be named Warmth In Fire," it answered with a note of melancholy.

There was such a pang within me that I had not felt in ages, for The Oneirotect was right. There was some years back, some centuries back, another Which Offers Heat And Warmth In Fire. And then, one day, there was not. They worked and strove and wept and bled over their chosen path, and then they were naught.

They—that other Warmth In Fire—was lost to us. They were gone from us. Their art took them from us, it killed them. Such is the danger of art, dear readers: it takes as easily—more easily!— than it gives. It was some centuries back, but- ah! Centuries change only the flavor of the loss when one cannot forget it. It is a loss that still stings to this very day.

"Ah," The Woman said, her expression falling subtly—nearly too subtly to notice, but by this point, I was quite focused on everything about her. "Right. I remember hearing of a death within the clade early on. Systime 54, was it? I was rather disconnected from the clade at the time, I am sorry to say, and was unable to focus enough to learn of just who."

I nodded. "But by then, Dear—or, rather the instance who would become Dear—had been forked, and so Warmth filled that vacancy. Ey took on the name Which Offers Heat And Warmth In Fire when Dear became what it is."

Warmth struggled to speak at first, caught up in emotion. It had been Dear at the time, and watched as who-was-Warmth descended into despair and, eventually, quit. Finally, it nodded, saying, "I am that which was left behind when Dear chose to forget the Name."

Now, perhaps my younger uploads or those who have not stuck their noses deep into cladistics, snuffling about for interesting thises or surprising thats, may not quite understand the import here, and so I will tell you a story, much as it was told to me by The Instance Artist:

Many years ago, it forked and went out for a walk along the street. It put the Name of our superlative friend, of The Dreamer who dreams us all, into an exocortex and then began to change. It forked and forked and forked as it walked that endless city that it called home at the time. It changed its shape, from stocky to slight. It changed its species. It changed its sense of smell, its sense of sight. It changed its hearing—and you must understand, as a fennec, its ears are enormous; when it gives a shake of its head, its tall ears bow under the momentum. It changed the way it thought about our history. It changed the way it thought about forking. It changed the way it engaged with everything around it.

Its goal was to change its sensorium enough that it would not be able to access the Name of our beloved Dreamer again.

Tired, it trudged back home. It could have simply stepped back, yes, but this was a part of the ritual. It had to see the way it had come through these new senses.

There was its back-up fork, sitting and reading and trying to distract herself from its absence. She looked like me, dear readers, yes? Back as I did then? Dear looked like me when it started, after all.

She looked up from her book, quirked a brow, and smiled.

"You may quit whenever," The Instance Artist had said. "I am happy now."

She stood, bowed, and shook her head, and then she stepped from the sim.

It did not see her for months after that. None of us did. Weeks and months of knowing that she was out there but knowing aught else aside from that.

It did not talk to her, friends, you must understand. It did not talk to her, and she did not talk to it, other than a notification that she would be taking the name Which Offers Heat And Warmth In Fire.

"I sat with a good book while it took that dire walk between skunk and fennec, and when it returned, it had become something unrecognizable to me. I could see the direction it took, but not the road it followed; it had become something alien, and the prospect of disappearing after that felt rather a lot more like dying than becoming, and so I chose to yield my name to it—for that Dear was that of me who had already become, yes?—and spent some months working to earn the name Warmth In Fire."

The Woman furrowed her brow in that ineffably still way of hers. "I remember that there was talk within the clade about names, yes, and the general shape of what had happened, that there was some furor about the fact that a down-tree might accept a later line than an up-tree, though I never did understand the import that some placed on that." There was a smile, a hint of a bow, and a quiet addition: "You are so incredibly yourself, though, I cannot picture you as ever having been a Dear, and certainly never as a fennec."

There followed a moment of The Oneirotect visibly mastering a note of annihilation upon hearing this. It was, I think, one of those things which hurts to hear, and yet which is completely right: ey is not yet another instance of The Instance Artist, nor has ey been for centuries, and yet there is that of The Instance Artist still within em, is there not? "When I stepped from that sim," ey explained, "I did so with the commitment, both to myself and to it, that what was Dear had changed, and that who was Dear must embrace that. I am unsure, however, that I have ever quite addressed the fact that, often when I hear about Dear from others, there is a rankling within me. Sometimes, when I am feeling particularly bad about myself, I feel like it stole my very name from me. I feel like a leftover, a shadow on the floor of the stage of my own show."

"The clade will ever be as it is," I said, tagging along with that thought, "which is a bunch of crotchety old creatures with a fixation on names that borders on neurotic. Do not doubt that this applies to our stanza as well."

The Woman smirked, nodded.

"There were those within the clade who fussed and fussed and fussed, and I would be remiss if I did not say that we had—and, as Warmth mentions, continue to fuss—about the role that names play in identity. We will ever be who we are, though, yes?"

My beloved up-tree spent some time pensively structuring its thoughts, trying to reclaim some sort of agency before it fell into a negativity spiral; such topics as these are always especially difficult for us to stumble across, and it had already started to recite some of those familiar phrases it so often repeats even to this day. "You have come to Rye and I searching for joy through creativity. I wonder: What do you imagine yourself to be, End Of Endings, other than the only one living there I get to call 'kitty' from time to time?"

The Woman laughed—and what a blessing a laugh is in comparison to a smile!—and, with no effort expended on her own part, fell right into that very shape: a kitty. Kitty! And what a delightful little name. You will remember, my friends, that not every instance of her changing shape was occasion for weariness or discomfort; she fell joyfully into felinity, into this pantherine shape. "I like that you call me kitty, my dear," she said, still smiling. "And I am always happy when I think of becoming such as occasion for you to do so."

It beamed, smug and sly and looking quite pleased for the change it had had a paw in working. It was very *not* Dear in that moment—it was (and is!) very Warmth In Fire because, while it shared some of that quippiness that Dear was so well-known for, Dear shared little of my 'motherly warmth', as it put it. Dear did not inherit such from me—or perhaps had lost it over long years with too many quips—but my beloved up-tree did.

Here was The Oneirotect being warm. Here was The Oneirotect being insightful and supportive. Here was her taking control for The Woman's sake. Here was it looking for some way to stop trauma-dumping on her and start guiding her closer toward self-understanding, toward a resolution, toward peace.

"But no, I imagine myself being other than just She Who Is Kitty From Time To Time. I imagine myself as someone who has found a purpose within her life other than, as Rejoice put it, simply being one who is built to suffer. Suffering may well be inescapable, but would that I were aught else than She Who Suffers."

"Is that what you feel you are now, my dear?" The Oneirotect asked, her tone veering further into direness once more, her words filled with ache and earnestness. "Do you not find joy in each day? Each hour? You, and all the others in that melancholy home of yours, have committed to perhaps the world's direst bit, but it is worth it, in the end, is it not? There is still tomorrow, and the opportunity it offers, is there not?"

The Woman sat with this in thoughtfulness, her expression perhaps now distant, perhaps now curious. Her gaze drifted from my beloved up-tree to me, and then somewhere over my shoulder, out toward the far wall, toward the door, and then panned once more over toward the windows, where the leaves of spring fluttered in a pleasant visual static.

When once more her eyes returned to us, her expression had settled into what, I do not know exactly. Pensive? Introspective? I cannot say, dear readers. I cannot say.

"I do feel joy, yes. I think that one of the things that sparked this train of thought was actually one such case of joy. I visited No Hesitation for a simple coffee date, and from there I was left with joy that lasted some few days. It was a comfort to me." The faintest of smiles turned up the corners of her mouth. "No, it was not just a comfort, it was a thing I clung to jealously, and when I felt that it was being slowly parceled out to others at home—for they too deserve joy—and when I was asked about it by Ever Dream, I felt as though it was slipping away from me with no recourse. Is joy to always do such? Every time I receive such joy, is it only to slip away?"

There was a sense then in The Oneirotect of discomfort at

this sentiment: that joy is fleeting. It had worked so hard to become able to appreciate the joys it had, despite the equally-ephemeral agonies it suffered at the hands of perfectionism and impostor syndrome—as do we all at times, yes?

"It will always be true that you shared that comfort together, End Of Endings," she said, my own maternal concern echoed in its voice, so many hours spent helping hold eir head above water while they wallowed in a spiral of self-loathing. "What is it that slipped away?"

"The..." The Woman started, then immediately fell off into silence. There was a frown on her face, though it was one of concentration rather than consternation. "What it feels has slipped away is the possibility of the permanence of joy, or even joy that lasts longer than suffering. I suppose that is what I am seeking in this exercise. I am seeking joy that lasts. Even if not forever, I am seeking joy that lasts. I am seeking intentionality in joy. I am seeking agency in joy."

My beloved up-tree was along for the ride up until the word 'agency,' at which it scrunched up its face and reared eir head back as though someone had—as often I have done—pressed on the tip of her little nose—or, it is not so little; it is a big honker of a schnoz as some cartoon might have. How often had ey struggled for its own agency? How often pawing feebly at a thing for years and years and feeling as if nothing it made met its own standards? How often wallowing and feeling helpless but to wallow? How often caught in a spate of ineffectual pining, of disinterest born of despair, of the sort of pain that festers and festers until she broke down into tears and overflowed? Ah–! But it replied, "Is the pain as well not itself as fleeting? Does it not fly away in the wind when a gust of joy blows your way? Does despair not crumble at the feet of relief, euphoria, pleasure? Is it not dashed away on the rocks of even one moment of the right kind of comfort?" It fell silent for a moment, gaze drifting outward toward those very same leaves as caught the Woman's eye. "It is still worth it, is it not? It must be worth it, or else all the world's a horror."

Here, now, was a moment of quiet between us all as The Oneirotect grappled with its silently tearful emotions. I have spoken of the ways in which we cry, the whys and wherefores, the shamelessness of it all, and so it grappled with its own whys and wherefores, its own shamelessness, and we—The Woman and I—looked on with curiousity and compassion and empathy, for we felt also some of these things.

Here, my friends, I must explain something. I must explain the Warmth In Fire before Warmth In Fire. I must explain The Sightwright who is no more.

It is as my beloved up-tree says: we also suffer. Have I not spoken of such? Of course I have! I cannot but! I cannot help myself in this.

The Sightwright suffered as I do, as The Oneirotect does, and perhaps even as The Woman did. It was so long ago that they left us, left me, and though I remember, I remember through the lens of centuries, through a glass, darkly. They suffered because of their art. They suffered because of the world around them. They suffered perhaps because we are all built to suffer.

They suffered as do my beloved up-tree and I, but they also suffered as did—I must explain, also, or perhaps remind—Death Itself and I Do Not Know.

They quit.

They suffered too much. They were, and then they were not.

I must explain and I must remind to set before you the context of what The Oneirotect said next.

My beloved up-tree's tears did not ebb before ey spoke. No, in fact, they flowed and flowed, a cascade of emotion trickling and then creeping and then washing across its face. I have spoken about the way I cry already, and, well, surely they got it from somewhere, yes? "There has been enough of death in the clade, my dear," it plead, wiping its eyes to no avail. Fur remained wet. Nose remained clogged. Voice remained round. Ey pulled eir paws away from eir face, looking appalled at the strands of spit and snot and salty tears. "You do not intend to quit, do you?" it croaked through another sob, voice small. "You will be with us for a good while yet, right? Please say yes."

The Woman smiled, and this smile was not a blessing but a benediction, and it was not for me but for solely The Oneirotect. It was my job only to witness this smile, this validation of pain. "No, dear one. I do not intend to quit." She let these words hang there in the air before us, a monument to such an intent. "No, I am seeking not just meaning but purpose. I have explored meaningful things and pleasurable things, but now I wish to explore direction."

The Oneirotect is not The Child, but my beloved up-tree is also my very own little one. With this comes at least some of the baggage of being small, including tears that seem to flow with an outsized force. So overcome by the base reality of a good, hard cry was it that ey could not help but laugh at emself. "Oh, good!" she managed, sucking back what ick she could. "I will hold you to that. If you quit, I will wipe this snot all over your headstone! It will cake itself between the grooves of your epitaph. It will dry there in the cracks and no dandelions will grow upon its stony bed; it will be the worst!"

At this, The Woman and I smiled. There perhaps was also room for laughter, but a simpler acknowledgment was required for now. A box of tissues was summoned. Glasses of water. Hugs and soft pets and gentle kisses between the ears such as might offer comfort. Such are the realities of a good cry, yes? The distasteful and the compassionate realities both? They are as worthy of acknowledgment as the reality of breath, sys-side. We do not cease being subject to our gross anatomy.

"A reminder: art is not strictly joy, but also suffering," I cautioned most gently. "With art comes fear. There is suffering of a sort in failure. There is suffering in falling short, as well; even if you succeed in an endeavor in your own eyes, you may feel the pain of lack." Despite her expectant silence, I held up a paw as though to forestall comments, for even movement is communication. "You are strong, End Of Endings, and I know—I think we know—that you are up to such a task, but I must remind you as well."

The Woman bowed her head, though whether in acknowledgment or a pensive shift in her thoughts, I could not tell. Perhaps it was both. Perhaps she felt then as I have so much lately: as though the world is not quite as it seems, as though there is something more beneath or above. Perhaps she felt keenly our superlative friend. "I understand, of course. I suppose that has also been the case in my explorations of late, that there ever be this balance." She lifted her head to smile wryly. "There is, as you say, suffering in many things, but the suffering of failure carries a particular tang of disappointment, does it not?"

The Oneirotect finally recomposed itself, reassured of The Woman's longevity. "Yes," she answered most bluntly. "Emphatically, yes. And yet, after nearly two and a half centuries, I am still doing it. Rye, you still write your stories, yes? Serene, she yet weaves her wilds, yes?" Its cadence fired up, its tone almost a challenge, daring End Of Endings to oppose this conviction forged in agony. "I still dream up my little wonders and Dry Grass still keeps them on her mantle and those who I will never know still greedily gobble their favored food from my work on the Exchange."

She paused, planting its paws between its knees to lean forward in eir seat. "There is vanity in art, and it is in vanity that we artists dwell. We mean to expose some part of ourselves, and there is torture in knowing *precisely* how wrong every act has turned out." The Oneirotect's fervor softened into something more familiar to me, more an expression of shared adversity than the bitter lesson of so many shattered dreams littering the waters in its wake. "That is why we must do this for more than ourselves, End Of Endings, why our art must have its own value lest we fall into the perpetual pursuit of some cruel point."

The Woman tilted her head—that habit that so often follows each and every one of us around like a little puppy. "You mean to consider my audience?"

I wobbled a paw. "While that is perhaps some of it—a great deal, even, as that validation does drive one on—there is more to art than that." I am not ashamed to say that I fall so easily back into that teacher mode of speaking. We were such for how many years, phys-side? And I have been such off and on for how many more, here? "You speak of purpose: it is also the sharing of what goes *into* art, too. I write for myself, yes, for the joy of it, and I write for others, too. But if my failures are instructive, then shall I not also pass that instruction on to others? I teach. I write *with* others. I read and give feedback."

At this she smiled. "Teaching has stuck with us, after all. You have already mentioned communalism, too."

"Yes, that is it!" The Oneirotect said, a bright smile plastered across its face. "Have we not all of us in our hearts our own little shrines to *communitas?* I want for every person on Lagrange to be able to do what we do, to weave dreams tangible or otherwise into being with the ease of centuries of experience. I want for them to enjoy the food of their lives back phys-side, to imagine what flavors the Artemisians indulge, to draw up from memory the last best moment they ever beheld. That is why I go with Jove and Why Ask Questions to their little skillshare, yes, but it is also why I have taken a liking to oneiro-impressionism. I do not want for this to be so hard for everyone forever.

"It is just as industry made our lives gentler, yes?" ey went on, tone shifting further into something perilously close to exhaustion. The pain it was tanking to explain itself to The Woman was plain to see on its face as it grappled with eir own doubts. It spoke with confidence to her, but The Oneirotect spoke also to itself, and I am proud to say that in the years that followed, this conversation proved fruitful for at least one of us.

"Let us discover some secret hidden in AwDae's little world," it mused, eyes steady on The Woman. "Let us find a way to render pedestrian what is, at present, an expert's privilege."

I am *proud* of em. I am as proud as any mother, as any attentive aunt, as any family member must be. They continually amaze me with just how much they have done with their life. She delights me with with her attentiveness to the audience of her art.

It, too, fills me with commiseration with its exhaustion, for such is also as I have felt in the ways that I move through the world and I move through my life and I move through my art. I have spoken and doubtless will speak yet more about my overflow, my graphomania, and will whine forever about the pain that comes with it, the feelings of inadequacy and lack when I consider as well that others will willingly read my words. Would that– ah! But I wander...

"I had not thought to question what art I might create provides to others," The Woman said after a silent moment's thought. "Now that I say that aloud, I am a little ashamed that I had not considered it. Much of this exercise that I have been undertaking has been focused on *my* joy, on what *I* might gain from being able to pick up from this or that, whether it be hedonism or love or art."

The sheepishness in her tone, dear readers, cut. I ached for her, even if she herself in that moment once more wore that blessed wry smile.

Beyond that, though, did I not also have thoughts on this? Did I not also have feelings on caring for oneself? The Golden Rule must also apply to oneself. We, too, deserve to be treated as we might treat others. It is the Silver Rule, perhaps, that the Golden Rule be inverted. Others are worthy of consideration when we think of our work, and yet...and yet...

And yet.

"It is no bad thing to consider those first, my dear," I said. "One must remember oneself first, though certainly not to the exclusion of others, of community. You cannot, after all, give to your community if you are unable to give, yes? The Golden Rule applies also to you, yes? You must treat *yourself* well, yes?"

She chuckled and gave a nod of acknowledgment. "Of course, Rye. I should not rush to judge this exploration so harshly this soon." Her shoulders sagged, then, and the ache within me swelled. "Perhaps I am simply sick of this suffering that Rejoice speaks of. Perhaps I am ready to move away from it. Not to quit, but to find some new basis for myself."

"And you are testing art as this new basis? Creating things, whatever that may be?"

She nodded. "I remain split on it, as yet. It is more complicated than I had imagined, given what you two have said, yes? It is much like Slow Hours's and Beholden's full-attention reading and listening. It takes the whole of me and is exhausting. I am exhausted even at the thought of starting."

I thought back to my first creations, to the first stories and poems and novels that I wrote, back when I was still learning how to forge and how also to hone, and laughed. "Oh, my dear, it is exhausting to *remember* starting. I will let you leave with one of my first stories. Thank goodness I did not allow it to see the light of day."

"That tiring, then?"

I nodded. "Beyond tiring. I do not know how it felt for Warmth, but for me, I would move in fits and starts, now loving my art and now feeling like it was trash, that I was treading already trod ground, that it was derivative. I suppose I had to learn how to learn, first, but even after that. I wanted to have become a great author, without going through the becoming part."

The Oneirotect snickered, resting a paw on my knee. "I had the advantage of your example to learn from," she started, looking to End Of Endings. "And my predecessor's. I *started* easily enough, but the despair of mediocrity ever tainted my motivation. That first week was full to brimming with excitement, that second worthy but deprived of euphoria, and on the third I inevitably stumbled into a wallowing spiral until the fourth, when I swore I would never try again, only for a new ambition to spring up the next." It shook its head, as though in disbelief at itself. I found it understandable, dear readers, and perhaps you do as well. Even after three hundred years, the ambition always returns. Perhaps it was not disbelief, then, that led my beloved up-tree to shake eir head, but a world-weary recognition of this—but I digress. "I have not improved very much at all in this respect; it is agony, but it has at least turned out to be sustainable. I only wish it did not *hurt* so much."

Furrowing her brow, The Woman looked down to her glass of water. "More complicated, indeed," she murmured, more to herself than anything—so evidently so that my beloved up-tree and I let her have that moment for herself, as though hesitant to interrupt it. "You speak of works you would not let see the light of day, Rye, and of the pain of creation. You both clearly still find meaning in it—as do Slow Hours and Beholden, of course, and Motes—so I am left wondering what one does with these feelings of...ah, I hesitate to say, but perhaps they are feelings of unworthiness. What does one do when one's works feel mediocre, especially if one is to create also for others?"

It took me some time to disentangle The Woman's words. They were starting to fall into a jumble, into a garden path of wanderings. Perhaps you may even sense that in me, friends, the ways in which my words wander, their circuitous routes, though I do not think that she was nearly so taken with language as I am, or at least not in quite the same way. I think she was simply tired. She certainly looked it, with the slump of her shoulders and the drowsiness in her features she nonetheless seemed intent on masking.

"I imagine it is different for every artist," I said most carefully, hesitant to in any way push The Woman away from any art she might wish to start. "For me, I keep all of my writing. I have exos full to overflowing with snippets and ideas, abandoned drafts, outlines I never got to. I am a bit of a packrat, in that way, and I am not sorry. I spoke before of learning to learn, and the utility of using that learning, and I think that is what I try to draw from them. There is that which I have created that only I value, yes, but its utility is in what it gives in improving going forward or in teaching."

The answer felt less than satisfactory, or perhaps not quite as true as it could have been, for there was work of mine that I loved for this utility and yet was unwilling to publish, not now, not work from when I was in the novitiate in my art. There is work of mine even now that I hate, that I loathe for, as The Oneirotect said, the wallowing spiral that spawned it and it makes me wonder, and at times it makes me tremble, that I must say there is worth in art when so much of mine feels worthless.

"End Of Endings, my dear," The Oneirotect said, slipping

down from her stool, "I am beginning to see myself in you, and that fills me with fear. You have promised me that you do not intend to quit, but if there *is* that of death in you, whatever art you choose will bring you perilously close to the brink time and time and time again." It padded up beside The Woman, placing both paws on her knees and looking up into her face. "Tell me, kitty, is it better to disappear into a blizzard, or should someone lay down their weary bones in a grave when they are through?"

The Woman has always been The Woman. This is the way of the world.

The Woman was born Michelle Rachel Hadje in 2086. On a March night, she was born. Anna Judith Hadje screamed and screamed and breathed and breathed and breathed and, with a gasp or sigh or groan or moan, Michelle graced the world, took a breath and, after a scant few seconds, wailed.

The Woman does not remember this, for how many of us remember our first breath, our first wail? She does not remember, but the fact is unassailable. From that point, she *was*.

The Woman was, for all intents and purposes, a normal, healthy child. She was wholly herself, and her parents loved her and her teachers teachers loved her and they all found her to be kind and empathetic, though prone to moodiness. "She is anxious," they said. "She is a people pleaser. She is autistic. She is bright and quick to laugh." And she was all of these things.

The Woman went to school, yes, as all unremarkable children do. Kindergarten came and went, and then grade school, where she sang and she danced and she acted in the little plays that grade-schoolers put on. High school then came, and it was there that she met RJ, and they fell in love, but it was not the love that leads to romance, though they at one point tried. They did what high schoolers who fall in love do and kissed behind the bleachers and held hands even at one point had a sleepover, where RJ's mom peeked in on them at midnight to make sure that they did little else beyond kissing and holding hands, but it had never been RJ's wont to do aught else. Even romance was beyond em, and it was not the fit for the two of them. They were instead in love that took the form of a superlative friendship. Perhaps they were soul mates, should such a thing exist, but if so, it was not the arrangement that led to romance.

The Woman, like so many other anxious and autistic and bright children, like so many people pleasers who are quick to laugh, spent much of her time online. Her parents, when she was fifteen, as soon as such was allowed by law, paid for the procedure to get her the implants that allowed her to delve in to the shared immersion that was a reality separate from the world. They paid for this because she sat them down and made the argument that she had found friends online, too, online where people glommed together into heterogeneous groups surrounding shared interests.

The Woman, you see, had picked up on furry as a subculture, for when you are a child with an active imagination that loves to play pretend, it is only natural to pretend to be an animal, yes? She pretended to be a cat, for she loved the way they moved, and she loved especially the way their shoulder blades would stick up above their spine as they prowled along, low to the ground. A house cat at first for one breezy year, and then a panther. Something larger, something sleeker, something with big, soft-padded paws that still kneaded while she purred. She was the panther who had named herself Sasha for reasons she could not quite articulate.

The Woman's superlative friend followed with her and then soon surpassed her. Ey picked not feline, but fennec fox, with ears too big and a brush of a tail and a short but pointy snout.

The Woman and her superlative friend moved together as one. They were the same person twice over, they would say. Michelle who was Sasha—a name chosen for who knows what reason—and RJ who was AwDae—a name that was a corruption of eir name—a name I feel no shame now in sharing. They were the pair who loved each other in their own way and who surrounded themselves with others. They were the pair who found each other and, when the world deemed them in some way unworthy of consideration, got lost together, for they fell among a crowd of politically active friends, as they were active themselves, and how inconvenient! Inconvenient people should be set aside, some bureaucrat thought. They should be put up high on a shelf in some forgotten storage. And so they were.

The Woman and her superlative friend, when next they clicked their implants into place and delved into the familiar second home that was the 'net, they were shunted away into dreams and left there to wilt, to languish, to desiccate and wither and be blown away by who cared what wind. They were knocked a meter to the right and back in some metaphorical way, their immersive tech refusing to relinquish its grip on their reality so that, from the outside, they only slept, and yet within, they dreamed along the filaments of those implants, trapped within that hardware, for the nature of getting lost was a coma mediated by integrated technology. They were both torn asunder in some ineffable way. For Michelle who was Sasha, those two identities were carved apart—though only halfway—and, when her superlative friend, her beloved RJ, gave of emself to create the world that was Lagrange, a System for those minds who chose to upload, she dove after em in as soon as she could afford.

The Woman and her superlative friend were ever bound up in each other, for they were the same person twice over, and since this world was in some ineffable way made *of* em, Michelle who was Sasha and The Woman who was Michelle felt she had no other choice, even if the unique trauma of getting lost meant that she ever felt that split, that inextricable Sasha-ness and Michelle-ness that someone, some bureaucrat that wanted her lost, inadvertently tried to reify, and it was not until the ability to fork—to copy oneself and multiply, to let instances merge back down or to continue on and become their own people—was added to the System that she was able to alleviate herself of such. Or, if not herself, at least she could ensure that those new copies of herself, the Ode clade, would be without such pain.

The Woman and her clade were never wholly without, for such is the way of trauma, yes?

But I digress.

×

The Woman wandered far from home. She picked a direction—east, if the entrance to that Gothic house on the field was due north—and began to walk. She walked for an hour. Then she walked for two, for four, for eight. She walked until the sun set and then she lay down in the grass and looked up to the stars and remembered all of these things and wept and smiled and laughed and sobbed.

She remembered these things, and I remember these things, just as I, in dreams, remember the sands beneath my feet and the rattle of dry grass in the wind and the names of all things and forget them only when I wake. She wandered the field and lay down and looked at the stars and bathed in memories and I pace the empty rooms of my home, listening to nothing, looking at nothing, clenching and unclenching my fists as I struggle not to reach for my pen, my paper, and instead write in my head.

Why do we so often do this? Why are there times when, over-flowing or not, we wrap ourselves up in our memories like the most comforting blanket in the world, and yet still cry? Why do we cry after loved ones? Why do we cry after ourselves? Why do we look up to the stars—stars we made!—and cry so bitterly? Why do the tears leave tracks in the fur on our cheeks or down over the skin of our faces? Why do birds, as the poet says, suddenly appear every time we feel such nearness as is left of our superlative friend?

The Woman lay in the grass of that sweet field arrayed in living green and dug her fingers down into the soil between the blades, clutching perhaps a dandelion.

When Michelle who was Sasha was lost, when she was set aside from the world as something undesirable, some anathema, she was placed within a dream and left to rot.

Within that dream, she saw a field very much like the one that The Woman now lay in, but also very much like so many other such fields sprinkled within Lagrange and Castor and Pollux, for we are many, are we not? We are, as we are so fond of saying, nominally one hundred, and yet we are thousands more, and so many of us have these fields, or perhaps snatches of field, that are speckled with dandelions. I have dandelions on the little moat of grass that surrounds my patio, just as did The Instance Artist who has since left Lagrange, but beyond the low fence that surrounds that patio lies a field, and that field is dotted liberally with them, and my beloved up-tree, The Oneirotect, will bring over her beloved friend, The Child, and they will race around yan tan tethera in endless circles, playing leapfrog or tag or simply running for the sheer joy of it and then go all atumble, and the white fur of their stripes will wind up streaked with the yellow of those dandelions and perhaps the green of that grass.

Within that dream, though, Michelle who was Sasha saw a field very much like the one that she lay in then, and her mind unwound and unraveled and began to fray and the sun rose and set and rose and set and rose and set and years passed and centuries passed and perhaps millennia, too, and then sixteen hours and twenty-three minutes later, she was lifted up up up out of the dream and set back into the real world, wobbly on her own two feet. The bureaucrat was arrested. The world heaved a sigh of relief, and then set about doing its best to forget her.

But The Woman who was Michelle who was Sasha would not let that happen. She *could not* let that happen. She and the others who were thus forcibly lost did not deserve to be lost again, forgotten by society, and nor did society itself deserve to forget that uncaring ones existed so prevalently. While she stayed as close to her superlative friend as she could, even after ey grew too terrified to delve in, to meet her as best they could as Sasha and AwDae, she campaigned for change, for greater protections from those who would view individuals as consumables to be chewed up and spat out

And then, one day, her superlative friend disappeared. Days went by, and weeks, and then before the month was out, she received a letter detailing the ways in which ey hoped to move forward, how ey would likely die, but at least ey would die in the act of creation, of making a new world of utter freedom, where dreaming together was the warp of the world, and intent the weft, and ey both succeeded and failed, for now the world in which we live is one woven from dreams and intent, but ey is absent. It was in that letter that ey had written the ode that became the source of our names, and so we live out our lives embodying these fragments of em, but even still, ey failed because ey is absent. Ey became the weaver.

And still, ey succeeded. Ey succeeded because ey became the loom while we became the fabric. Ey became the shuttle and the pirn and the batten and the comb and the heddle, and the world is the lathe and we are the treadles working and working and working and we feel em beneath our fingertips as they trace along the weave, but ey is not here.

But I digress.

×

We are built to love, The Woman and I and all of our kin, and do not let any of us or anyone else try to convince you otherwise, for we *all* are built to love. We are built to love and to be loved.

We are also built of trauma, The Woman and I and all of our kin. We are built of trauma on trauma on trauma, and trauma and trauma. We are stacked brick by brick. We are built with logs stacked in a square, notches cut to make them fit. We are cabins. We are houses. We are buildings and skyscrapers. We are wobbly towers. We are smokestacks in the wind, and when the air passes over us a clockwise vortex will form and then a widdershins vortex and then a clockwise vortex and the air is life and the air is time and the vortex shedding tugs and pulls at us until we topple.

We must consider the most obvious trauma of them all, yes, when Michelle who was Sasha and her superlative friend were transitively lost, along with however many hundreds of others, but we are not defined solely by that, are we? No one is defined solely by one thing. We are fully realized people, just as you and you and you and you and you are, dear readers. If you were to come up to me at some reading, some book signing, and say to me, "Rye! You have told me of the time that The Woman came to your house and had that conversation that changed you in so many subtle ways, and you have told me of getting lost. Those must be the defining moments of your life," I would say to you, "You are forgetting that dinner that I had with The Instance Artist and its partners, and The Oneirotect, and The Sim Artist, where we ate so many wonderful foods and yet they all sat like lead in my belly as we realized that there was death in the air and death on The Instance Artist's tongue, for Launch was only a week away and to us it would be dead, and you are forgetting so many other joys and fears and so many other little traumas that make me *me!*"

We are built of trauma, and trauma and trauma on trauma and trauma and trauma, all stacked high like some wobbly tower, some smokestack that twists in the wind and then comes apart in overflow, The Woman and I and all of our kin.

The Woman was overflowing on that field, there, laying in the grass and flowers, staring up at the stars and the faintest outline of a new moon, laughing and weeping, far more herself than anyone person has any right to be, herself pressing against her chest from the inside, aching, rising up in her throat like bile, and I am overflowing right now, you see, or close enough to it, for even now, as I pace the empty rooms of my house, listening to nothing, looking at nothing, with my paws clenched into fists so that I do not grab my pen and paper to write and instead write this in my head, I feel how much of me there is, the way it aches, the way it presses against my chest from the inside and rises in my throat like bile, and I wonder what will become of me.

But I digress.

×

We are built to love, yes, The Woman and I and all of our kin, and how complicated that is!

What is one to do when faced with the enormity of love? What subtle powers does such wield over one? Are we beholden to the fact that we deserve love? Had we not deserved love, were we not to deserve love, what would become of us? Would we be better off by choose-your-metric? Would I be better off if I could love beyond that familial love I feel for those in my stanza, for those in my clade? If I felt feelings of romance of desire of libido of attraction of soul-mate-ness of this-ness or that-ness would I be better off, or am I better for lacking such?

The Woman and I and all of our kin have not always had the best of luck with love, nor with standing up for ourselves. When I say that we have more traumas than simply getting lost, our unluck in love accounts for some sizeable portion of this.

We struggled with the role that our bodies played, yes? For Michelle who was Sasha was short—as we are—and she was fat—as many of us remain—and she was so-called blessed with breasts to match; so called by those who wished to in some way claim ownership of them. When she pursued a reduction, her back thanked her and those who bestowed such praise wondered why why why she would withhold that goodness from them.

And yet even that did not stop such attention, for we were, it seems, worth a certain set of things to others—to those beyond our friends and our superlative friend with whom we remain in love—and so why would they hunt for aught else?

We are skunks for a reason. We bear these aposematic stripes for a reason. We adopted them to say: stay away. I am no longer worthy of such.

We also bear these scars on our chest for a reason: a reclamation. We found new joy in this transgression on the gender we are told is worth X and Y and Z. We are more than short fat women—though we also find joy in that—for What Praise exists, yes? My cross-tree? Lovely, he is. And Deny All Beginnings exists, yes? Trans man that he is? And Hold My Name exists, yes? Tall and trans and woman the long way around and transgressive for it? There is queerness in us and *that* is the more that we love, that is the A and B and C that is not the X and Y and Z.

We are skunks for a reason and we bear these aposematic stripes to also say: stay away. I am as I am and I will not be anything else.

It worked some of the time.

But I digress.

×

We are skunks for a reason and we bear these aposematic stripes for a reason and we bear these scars on our chest for a reason and we also bear these scars on our thighs for a reason. Should you, dear, dear friends, be so thoroughly plagued by self loathing that the only option to move forward is to externalize that pain, that hatred of self, through blood through a knife through a hot wire pressed to flesh, then can do naught else but beg you not to.

There is reclamation to be had there, yes, for so many of us have kept those subtle ridges on our thighs, marking skin or easily felt through our fur, because they are a part of who we are entirely. I still bear them and will not fork them away.

There is also reason not to keep them, for we have moved beyond what we were, and that, too, is a loveliness for its very truth.

I do not know whether The Woman bears these still. I do not *know*, gentle readers, much about her. I do not know if she *actually* went out and walked east from the house for hours and hours and a day and lay down in the grass and dug her claws down beneath the roots and stared up to the stars and laughed and wept. I will say that she did.

Enough digressions.

We are all of us beings of balance. We live with one foot in two worlds. We live with our thoughts in life and in death. We live with our hearts here and also there. We are platonic minds and bodies, and we are unified in the both of them in a Blakean energetic hell.

We are those who have scars because we sought the self-fulfillment of a breast reduction and those who have scars because we hurt so much we took a knife or a hot wire to our skin where such might be easily hidden. We are these things because we love life with a ferocity that leaves others breathless and also, though there is only the faintest whiff of suicidality in us, yearn in some intangible way for that which is not life, whether it be void or rest or, yes, joy.

I feel that call now, yes, as I pace the empty rooms of my home, listening to nothing, looking at nothing, clenching and unclenching my fists as I struggle not to reach for my pen, my paper, and instead write in my head, and perhaps The Woman felt that, too, as she wandered east and lay down in the field and looked up to the stars and held in her paws that other, most peaceful life that plants dwell within.

And yet I feel that fearful love of life within me now, for the words that I am writing now, pacing my empty house without senses but those bound up in my mind, stroke most softly along some part of me that is built to love, a silk dragged along skin and a soothing balm on bothersome scars and a cooling ice that runs through my veins to calm the fire of graphomania as though they were not actually a symptom of such, and perhaps The Woman felt that, too, as she overflowed beneath the stars and felt growth and growth and growth and growth and growth and growth beneath her paws and between her pads as blades of grass and achingly beautiful dandelions reached for the heavens where perhaps our superlative friend dwells.

Enough digressions.

The Woman is *whole,* my beloved friends, my dear readers. She is *whole!* She is *whole!* She has to be whole. I tell you, she is *whole.* I tell you as I write this with tears streaming down my face and blood soaking my paws from the way that my claws dig into my palms that she *has* to be whole. For all of our sakes, for *my* sake, she has to be whole she has to be whole she has to be whole I have to be whole she has to be whole I have to be whole for otherwise what will become of me?

×

When at last The Woman returned home, left my home and returned to her own, walked out into the field for a day and then lay down, her mind was aswirl with possibilities and all the various endlessnesses thereof. She felt full. She felt *overfull.* She felt as though she had had poured into her several depths, oceans of possibilities and each as deep or deeper than the last. She was vast. She was limitless. She was these things, and yet she was infinitely smaller than the limitless endlessness of the void which still lay within and without.

She returned home after that talk with me and my beloved up-tree, with your humble narrator and The Oneirotect, and she went for a walk and she did that which she is good at: she napped. There, out on the grass, there, she napped.

My dear, dear friends, the longer I go on, the more I pace around through quiet rooms the more these words swirl around me in some quiet maelstrom, the more I wish that I could do the same. Sleep brings no relief. Within my dreams there are yet more words. The boundary between waking and sleeping is so faint, now—I write even in my sleep! My dreams are of The Woman! My dreams are of me sitting at my desk with my pen in my paw and paper before me, of ink on page and words flowing after like an eager puppy!—the boundary is so faint now that I have more than once awoken from uneasy sleep to found that I had indeed at some point sat down at my desk and written word after word after word, after word and word and word. I have found pages of endlessly repeating phrases. I have found scribbles that are doubtless words and yet which I cannot decipher, and I cannot remember my dreams well enough to say what they may have been.

Did The Woman dream, we may wonder? Did she lay down and sleep after that conversation and look up to the constellations in the fabric of the sky, close her eyes, and then let play within her head some scene, some dream within a dream within a dream within a dream, some stream of meaning that the subconscious mind as dreamed by The Dreamer of the world dreamed forth?

I do not know.

Let us suppose she had, though! Let us take a look at what has made up The Woman so far and extrapolate some perhaps dream.

When first we began, when first some saner me set pen to paper or claws to keyboard, The Woman was set within her ways. She was set, as with her cocladists within her stanza, as one of those who suffers. She had hopes for moving forward with her life, yes, and dreams, but there was some part of her that fell in alignment with Her Cocladist's assessment that it was her lot in life as a member of the tenth stanza to provide a client for the seventh, those therapists among us. That was the moment when I began this story, telling of who she was, of expressing her as she might express herself, as did Collodi with Pinocchio: once upon a time there was not-a-king.

For she is our Pinocchio, is she not? She is our Pinocchio in reverse. She is the one who was born into this world too real and yet yearned for some of the stillness of so-called-inanimate wood.

The Woman then had her inciting incident, did she not? She had that moment when she met with Her Friend and felt after some form of joy that she could not quite put into words, and with that joy, against that joy, she felt the loss of joy over time, the way it was secreted within the treats that she delivered quietly to her cocladists and the way it seemed to trickle out of her life. And the second part of this incitation was the way that this fading of joy was cast against the stasis of her stanza, the suffering supposedly bestowed upon them. It showed to her plainly the impermanence of such joys, and thus, by omission, the possibility of a permanent pleasure.

She is and we are of a neurodivergent type, and so her approach to hunting for such joy as she imagined was of such a type as that: thorough and curious, methodical and whimsical. She set before herself by rule of fives five investigations: food, sex, entertainment, creation, and change. The first four of these brought joy, and even superlative joy, but not the joy she sought, not the stillness she sought, and before her lay the prospect of change, and yet such a prospect was exhausting before she had even begun.

And so now we may only guess at the dreams of one such as her, one who lives within our consensual dream, one who is dreamed by The Dreamer who was at one point our superlative friend.

Here is my supposition:

The Woman went walking. In her dream, she went walking, though it was not out on her field, the one we have seen so often. No, instead she went walking out her bedroom and through her secret door, out through the door and onto the street of the city that had become so familiar to her over the years, that city with the brick pavers and the fallen leaves which skittered so anxiously around her feet. She went walking in her dream and made her way through unnervingly empty city streets, walking and walking and walking. She passed the trolley stops. She passed the coffee shops. She passed, perhaps, the setting sun.

And at some final point—final!—she came across a square set within the cement of the sidewalk perhaps two meters on a side where the concrete gave way to a metal grate in the form of a sunburst, and in the middle there was a circle of soil, good and clean.

There, within her dream within a dream within a dream, she smiled. She smiled and she sank slowly to her knees in that ritual circle described in steel and dug her fingers down into the soil. Down and down and down she pushed, and as she did, she felt her fingers lengthen, stretching and twisting, seeking nutrients and water, seeking final—final!—purchase. They twisted and stretched down as roots and spiraling up her arms was a texture like bark and the bones of her neck and back elongated and her eyes sought *HaShem* or The Dreamer or some greater void and her hair greened to that of leaves and drank thirstily of the sunlight.

Finally—finally!—with one orgasmic flush of joy, The Woman became The Tree, and there was a joy everlasting in such stillness.

This is my supposition because this is my dream. This is a world I have seen and a world I have dreamed and it is a world that I have found a way still to love, even after it turned in on itself and ate so many of its own, even as The Dreamer who dreams us all stumbled and skinned eir palms and elbows on the brick pavers of this land. Since I have become myself, since your humble narrator was first called Dear The Wheat And Rye Under The Stars, that has been my dream. I have put it in verse. I have put it in prose. I have put it in story—this story. I have dreamed hundreds of times over the centuries that I have lived that I, too, fell to my knees and dug my fingers into the soil and became, in some pleasure-bound process, something still and sky-reaching, something earth-eating and water-drinking.

This is my supposition for The Woman and her dream after she came home from my house, because I think within her all along was that stillness, that sky-reachingness and earth-eatingness and water-drinkingness.

×

The longer we live—and, my dear readers, I will remind you that I am now 323 years old!—the more evident it becomes to us that there is a fractally cyclical nature to life: the years spiral up and the months spiral around and the days spiral forward—weeks are a construct borne out of our inherited faith but perhaps they too spiral—and so we live within a fractally cyclical tangle of time.

I know this. You know this, I am sure, on however instinctual a level, for you are clever and bright and you see the world with fresher eyes than I have. You are cleverer and brighter and fresher than your humble narrator who paces the empty rooms of her house and fills them with the quiet muttering of the mad.

The Woman knew this as well. When she woke from her nap—for my astute readers remember that that is how this rambling chapter began!—she could now—in a way she could not before—feel and perhaps even see these spirals. She could see the way that her 317 years had spiraled up around her. She could see the way that time bound her, tied her up in coils and coils and coils and coils and coils. She could see these coils—however metaphorically—as they twined around her legs and torso. She could feel these coils—however metaphorically—slowing her down, holding her arms to her side and limiting her reach. They—these coils and coils and coils—obscured her.

Ah, my friends, I am struggling. I can feel and see these coils and coils and coils and coils and coils and coils and coils and coils, yes, and am obscured.

I am going to lay down, and perhaps I will dream.

x

I have slept now. I took a cue from The Woman and took a nap, and while it did not come quite so easily to me as it ever did to her, it still offered some respite.

I dreamed, though! I dreamed of words like leaves and sentences like branches and stories like trunks, standing solid, with premises like roots dug into logic like earth and drinking of emotions like water. There was the tree, yes, for there was the green of the words and the brown of the story and the deep darkness of logic and emotion.

And above was the sun which was also The Dreamer who dreams us all.

When at last The Woman returned home from her walk of hours and hours and a day, she performed a new ritual. She performed a ritual of mourning.

This, you see, was the first pawings at her final task. Her set of five tasks, of food, of physical pleasure, of entertainment, of creation, of change was not quite complete, and had within it one more step, and she felt most a connection to the spiritual in the act of mourning and hoped in that to seek change.

My friends, I think it may well have been our conversation, that of The Woman and The Oneirotect and I, that set her mind thus in motion, for was it not then that we spoke so freely of my beloved up-tree and the way it mourned over Should We Forget? Did not the pair of long lost tenth stanza lines come up as well? Death Itself and I Do Not Know? They, too, perhaps felt some of this too-full-ness that The Woman struggles with, for back and back and back and back and back and back, six decades back, they lay still in thought and, before long, before the week was up, quit. They bowed out. They dipped. Committed suicide. Quit the big one. They push now up some perhaps daisies perhaps dandelions perhaps columbines perhaps nasturtiums in the mind of The Dreamer who dreams us all.

There is loss in our lives and in our hearts and in our minds.

But the tenth stanza knows *these* losses with a particular keenness. They leave empty seats and full plates at the table for these three who are gone. They speak the names of the dead on at least their Yahrzeit when they light the candle, and, for some of them, far more often, for The Woman's Cocladist was very fond of Death Itself, as the two loved each other fiercely, and it was perhaps this loss that drove Her Cocladist's bitterness and aught-elses.

Friends, you must understand that *we* love *us*. Even those of us who bore hatred for the others, the hatred of much of the sixth and seventh stanzas for others within the clade, even they love *us*. Some of us just bear a particular love for others of us. I have my beloved up-tree, yes? And ey has eir trickster partner, yes? And My Friend has The Musician, yes?

*We* love *us*, and The Woman's Cocladist loved Death Itself.

And so The Woman walked quietly up the stairs and knocked on Her Cocladist's door.

"Come in," came the quiet reply.

The Woman pushed the door open and bowed. "Rejoice."

"Ah, End Of Endings," Her Cocladist said from the amorphous chair she had claimed as her own, a perch over by the window where she read. Beside her: a stack of books. Behind her: several more. Lining the walls of the room: shelf after shelf after shelf after shelf of books. Shelf after shelf after– ah, the words fit so poorly, and so I try again and again and again to write them again.

"May I join you for a few moments?"

"Of course. What brings you to the end of the hall?"

"I would like to sit by Death Itself's bed for a few minutes."

Her Cocladist, halfway through setting her book aside, froze, and a wash of skunk spiraled up along her form, only to be replaced yet again by humanity, black fur sprouting, wilting, fading, leaving only skin. "Why?"

The Woman stood still in the doorway. "Because I am sad, and because I miss her."

"Alright," Her Cocladist said and finished the act of setting her book down, tented over the open page—no, do not get angry at her; sys-side, there are no broken bindings. "Do not sit on her bed."

The Woman bowed once more and stepped at last over the threshold, shutting the door behind her.

Along the other wall—that wall that had been hidden to the woman—was a simple bed, a single bed, a single-size mattress, and a wall painted in a feathery ombré from golden orange to purple-black. The covers were rumpled, clearly slept in. Clearly slept in and also clearly frozen in time, for the bed had not been touched since Death Itself had quit fifty seven years before. The Woman would not sit on it, even had Her Cocladist not warned her, for such was simply the way of things. The same was true of I Do Not Know's bed, and the only person who had laid in Should We Forget's bed was The Oneirotect who deserved such an expression of grief.

The Woman had her own ritual of grief to perform, though, and this did not call for touching the bed.

Instead, she sat down near the end of it, across the room from Her Cocladist, for both beds had at their feet matching beanbags—when you have a tail that flickers into being at moments not under your control, you are limited in your seating, you see, to the types of seats that can accommodate such caudal majesty that skunks sport—where once Her Cocladist and Death Itself would sit at times and talk and share in kindnesses such as touch when their forms permitted.

There, The Woman remained still.

She had within her an idea that there was mourning to be had in proximity.

She had within her an idea that there was change to be had in mourning.

She had within her an idea that there was stillness to be had at the end of change.

She figured that if proximity allowed her to mourn and mourning allowed her to process, and processing was a change that might bring her to stillness, here, *here,* there was a chance at a hint of a taste of this potential.

And besides, perhaps there was stillness in prayer. While Michelle who was Sasha inherited the faith of her parents and grandparents before them of Judaism, she herself did not inherit much of such from Michelle who was Sasha—this was the realm of the third stanza, of Oh But To Whom and Rav From Whence and What Right Have I—and yet the kernel of such lives within us all for thus is the nature of an inherited faith.

And yet regardless of her faith, there are, I am told, four kinds of prayer: words of thanksgiving, words of supplication, words of wonder, and the silence of meditation. I think, though, and perhaps you may think as well, that there are words of woe, of distress, of pain and fear and of the yearning for something—*anything*—when our *HaShem* does not feel near.

I think The Woman, as she sat across from Her Cocladist and watched how she looked now out the window, unseeing, silent tears coursing down her cheeks and leaving tracks on cheeks or marks in fur, leaned hardest on the last. One might think that she would in her seeking of stillness lean harder on the silence of meditation but I also think that it hurts too much to witness some pains. The Woman was kind. She was empathetic. She could sit there in pain with Her Cocladist and pray: how long, *Adonai,* will You forget me always? How long hide Your face from me? How long shall I cast about for counsel, sorrow in my heart all day? Regard, answer me, *HaShem,* my God. Light up my eyes, lest I sleep death. My heart exults in Your rescue my heart exults in You my heart exults in You my heart exults in You my heart exults in You my heart–

Perhaps this is how she prayed, perhaps this is how I pray. Perhaps I cast about for something—*anything*—to anchor me to *this* world, to *this* reality, to *this* life and call out: why am I forgotten? Perhaps I do my best to trust. Perhaps I do my best to cause my heart to exult in some god in whom I am not sure I believe that I may be regarded, that I may be answered.

Perhaps that is not how she prayed. Perhaps she rested her cheek on her fist and looked as well out the window and cried, or perhaps not, but still she sat in silence. Perhaps she leaned not on psalms of anguish but on the silence of meditation

Perhaps she did not pray at all and sought only to grow beyond that which she was by internalizing this loss. I do not rightly know, and can only surmise.

Perhaps she, like me, like Job, struggled with maintaining a faith disinterested in reward or punishment or relief from sorrow. Perhaps she, like me, wished she could believe in the hope that such disinterested faith might still provide a soothing balm against pain. Perhaps she, like me, struggled not to fall into the cynicism of Qohelet, the gather of the assembled who mused aloud: I set my heart to know wisdom and to know revelry and folly, for this, too, is herding the wind. Who mused aloud: what gain is there for man in all his toil that he toils under the sun? Who mused aloud: everything was from the dust, and everything goes back to the dust.

Perhaps she spoke to The Dreamer who dreams us all, perhaps not, but either way, she did not find stillness in the keenness of sorrow, nor spirituality in the change wrought by mourning, nor aught else but pain in the unending stasis of Her Cocladist, looking now out the window, unseeing, silent tears coursing down her cheeks and leaving tracks on cheeks or marks in fur.

×

The Woman sat down on the floor by The Dog some days later, a week later. She knew he was a cladist, for cladists come in many shapes—did she not also appear as a skunk? And a panther? And now, here, she was a human!—and so hoped he might have insight into unbecoming. This, after all, was the purpose of her visit to Le Rêve, the neighborhood of the fifth stanza, that of The Poet and The Musician and My Friend, and also The Child. It was The Child who was her goal, you see. She wished to speak with those who had changed, who had pushed themselves into new molds, who had become something new, that they might no longer be what had once drove them. Stillness lay in choice—that was the thought she held onto—that is the thought that I wish I could believe; would that I could choose to be still! Would that I could choose silence and images instead of yet more words.

The Dog had attached himself to Au Lieu Du Rêve, to the theatre troupe and to the fifth stanza, to His Skunks, some time ago. He spent many lazy days among them, many evenings dozing by the kettlecorn stand in the theater lobby in the hopes of someone dropping their snacks, many frantic minutes carrying The Child's latest core dump to the resident systech after she yet again in a bout of play had crashed.

The Dog was the fork of a systech, itself. No longer a systech, primarily a dog, but with such a drive within it. It, like its fellow dogs, lived a simplicity that Its Elder found himself wishing for now and again, but it still felt that sense of duty to people and the world. How very canine of it! How very companionable! Friendship is stored in the dog, yes? It did not know if it would ever grow weary of its role and return to Its Elder, or perhaps cast away what remained of its desire to do anything but exist as itself.

"I want to change. I want to unbecome," The Woman said to The Dog, crouching down where it lay, curled in sun, curled on a cushion so thoughtfully provided. "I want to become still. I came to speak with Motes, but you have done a similar thing, and I want to understand."

The Dog heard these words. He understood, I think, that he

was being asked about how he became himself. He knew he could think about these things, could answer, could take up a larger piece of his buried humanity and become a being of words and such actions. He did not want to do this, but he did not *not* want to.

It rose. It walked in front of the kettlecorn machine. It sat. It raised its front paws to beg. It was certain its intent was clear.

The Woman made a bag of kettlecorn and held out a piece to The Dog. He accepted, of course. What dog would not?

"*Practice and wanting,*" The Dog responded via sensorium message.

"Practice?" The Woman asked, lowering herself down to once more meet The Dog on its level.

The Dog did not answer, but sniffed in the direction of the corn.

The Woman gave The Dog another piece, for this was, evidently, the deal. "*I remember,*" The Dog said. "*The tall one wanted to eat and chase and fetch and be. He wanted to not worry, to not tire himself out chasing making the world better. But he couldn't just become me, become us—The Job is important.*"

The Dog waited for another bribe before continuing, for this was, evidently, the deal. "*He practiced becoming the pack, becoming like me. I remember many forks of his. Some that didn't let go enough, some that let go too much. But he wanted to make me, make the pack. He kept wanting, kept trying, and now I am.*"

The Dog yawned. He had said a lot of words, and that was not always comfortable for him. It is not comfortable for me, yes? I am a being of words and words and words and words and it is uncomfortable, my friends, so uncomfortable. It reminded The

Dog too much of human things, of things he no longer was in some integral way. He wanted a nap.

"'Let go too much'?" The Woman asked.

*"Some of us forget our job,"* The Dog explained.

"Job?"

The Dog's tail wagged. *"Yes! I watch and if someone becomes a black ball or the ground goes weird or something like that I fetch help! It's very important! When I do it, people call me a good dog and give me pets and treats!"*

The Woman reached out to pet The Dog. It relaxed into the pressure.

*"Some of the pack decide they don't want the job, want to do what the tall one is afraid of. They want to never talk, never plan."*

"I want something like this, perhaps," The Woman said. "I want to be still, to unbecome. Do you know how?"

The Dog froze in a swelling of alarm. His fears came from the same simplicity as his joys. While he was wont to let the possibility of casting off his humanity sneak up on him slowly, he still felt fear, like His Elder did, at such a blunt statement of the idea. *"Don't want! Who will watch Motes?"*

The Woman gently soothed The Dog, letting the interaction fade away behind a stream of pets and scratches in just the right spot (for The Dog knew how to direct people to it) and yet more treats. We are creatures of pleasure all, you see. The Woman and I, yes—for do we not both like being brushed?—but also the rest of our clade and so many others besides. What pleasure there is in rending the mind from the body and letting it live as it will! What pleasure! What pleasure there is in choosing a form one inhabits entirely! What pleasure! What pleasure there is in living for decades and centuries! What pleasure! The Dog was pleased that The Woman had not been told by Its Skunks not to feed it too much kettlecorn, or that, if she had, she was ignoring them.

Once The Dog had come down from being ambushed by the thought of abandoning those principles he had carried into his state, he realized what The Woman had wanted. *"Can show you pack-friends who go chase rabbits all the time. But no words because they don't want. And can't say how. Don't want to know."*

"Good dog. Thank you," The Woman said, and pet the dog some more. "Good dog. Good dog."

The Dog lit up. It *was* a good dog!

The Woman saw this and had a thought. "Are you happy?" she asked, handing over one more kernel. "Are you at peace?"

The Dog had made himself into a dog, more or less, and so was not one to consider the path of his life with much reflection or weight. He was rarely a creature of the past or the future.

*"Happy? Yes! Have treat!"* The Dog leapt up and started doing little hops, having realized it had an opportunity. *"Throw ball? Then, very happy!"*

The Woman could tell this was all the answer she would get for now. A ball appeared in her hand.

The Woman threw. The Dog fetched, and in that moment, in that place, there was peace.

×

The Dog took then The Woman to a forest, and showed her where The Rabbit-Chaser lived. There, The Dog went to greet The Rabbit-Chaser. He sniffed it, as is custom among their species, and it sniffed back.

The Rabbit-Chaser went to investigate The Woman, for here was a new thing by its den. The Woman gave it kettlecorn, which it ate before wandering off. The day was warm, and it was sleepy and not hungry, so it ignored The Woman and returned to its nap.

The Dog left. He knew it was close to dinner time, and he had plans to hover around one kitchen or another, for if we who have uploaded are hedonists, if our clade is a clade of hedonists, then the fifth stanza has set themselves as the hedonists *ne plus ultra.* If, my friends, you ever have the chance to visit them for one of their many cookouts or to get invited over for one of their many feasts, do take it up. They are lovely cooks and yet lovelier conversationalists, though this, I think, was less The Dog's focus than such treats that The Child managed to sneak him when My Friend and The Musician were not looking.

The Woman watched The Rabbit-Chaser as it saw to its immediate concerns. Food, yes, and sleep, water. Perhaps it would play with some of the other animals in these woods if the mood struck, or perhaps it would lounge in the sun until it got too hot, panting and panting and panting, and then pancake in the shade, drawing coolness from the ground itself.

It was what it was right then and nothing else. The Woman could sense, from her long, meditative observations, that The Dog and The Rabbit-Chaser were not quite the same, that The Rabbit-Chaser had shed more of its cares.

It explored a forest, sometimes running, sometimes sniffing thoughtfully, without a plan.

It prepared for tomorrow, if it absolutely must, by instinct and routine, or perhaps it did not.

The joys and tragedies of its home drifted past its mind and into its too-perfect memory. Loves! Pleasures! Sorrows! Lives! Deaths! The laments of starving wolves outmaneuvered by deer! The blood of deer ripped to shreds by wolves! It did not determine what of what its eyes, ears, nose, tongue, paws took in was good, was evil, was just, was improper—it beheld what was, not what ought be, and there was a peace in that.

It experienced each moment as it came and moved on, not stopping to analyze or categorize or name.

It was a dog, as much as it could be.

It had not always been a dog. It had a down-tree, the tall one who smelled of pack, who the word-users call Tomash. It had come from Its Elder when he had been experimenting with not only taking the shape of a dog but something of the mind as well.

It had been Scout, then, when it first came to be. When Its Elder had forked too well, too firmly, and it had not minded the name then. It had gone to simply be in the world, and it was, and is.

At first, it had had some occasional care for humans and the System, but it was hard to care when there were so, *so many* other things: new scents! Food! Scratching an itch! All of these were very important things when you are a dog, and they are important now. Here. Vestigial, inherited cares were a problem for later.

Then it had met the rest of its relatives, that growing pack of Scouts who rested within the System and experienced it, but who, unlike The Rabbit-Chaser, had a purpose: to keep watch and observe, and to report unusual things, and to, when they grew bored of being a dog, merge back. It liked these new relatives well enough—they smelled of family and were friendly—but it had not liked what they represented. They hesitated at becoming what they were, and it had understood that it might become more like them if words and thoughts and worries were to trouble it.

So, it rejected them.

Oh, the whole of its clade were welcome to visit and play, but it had told them, when it had cleared its name to as nothing as it could manage, a blank, a zero-width joiner, something unspeakable for the word-users, something unreadable, it had told them that it wished to hear not another word. It would not be communicating about anything that could not be said with the twitch of an ear or the wag of a tail, and it pushed away the slow stirrings of memories of personhood with a fork to ensure it.

The pack respected its wish. It saw them, sometimes, usually the young or the old who come to rest more thoroughly, and they played and ran and said nothing. What was there to say, after all, to this dog who surrendered thought with every step of every day?

When the pack spoke of it among themselves, in their fragmentary network of passed-around words and sensoria impressions, it was called Scout Chasing Rabbits, the far pole of the clade, the pure contrast to Their Elder, the other extreme. It did not know they said this. It did not want to know they said this—nor, by now, want to *not* know it; it worried not of *knowing* and it was happy thereby.

And in the bliss of not-knowing, through unwitnessed years and decades, it slept and ate and chased rabbits.

The Woman could not tell which of them had it better, these two dogs, these two cladists, these two beings who had so distanced themself from what they had once been. Both seemed quite content with the path that had taken. Dogs! What wonders they are! What pleasures! What joys. They had both unbecome, or taken steps in that direction, in their own way, and had found what they wanted.

This was close, dear readers! This was so close to what she sought. This worrying not of *knowing* was so close, but the Woman realized even then that, for her, the life of an animal, even one so invested in its state as The Rabbit-Chaser, was not what she sought, not quite, not exactly. It did not go far enough. It was not *still* enough. The her who was a beast would still have too much of her, too many cares and worries and too much of herself.. The her who was a skunk or a panther was still an active entity, an agent of her own future. In the end, the she who was these things was still an actor. She needed a change more integral, more whole, more entire—not a reshaping of the body, nor even the mind, but a reshaping of the existence.

So, her search continued.

×

She met then with The Child after this diversion—for such was her errand, yes? This was her original reason for visiting the neighborhood, and she saw no reason not to continue along this path. She returned to the lobby of the theatre which served also as a community center for Au Lieu Du Rêve, the troupe in which the fifth stanza had embedded itself, long familiar despite her having never seen it—for, you see, Michelle who was Sasha was a theatrician before uploading, a teacher, a director, an actress. Theatre lobbies smell like theatre lobbies and theatre carpet underfoot feels like theatre carpet underfoot and the sound echoed precisely as she had always remembered it.

Outside shone the sun. Outside grew the grass. Outside was the dusty gray of the asphalt street that wound around the center of this neighborhood—a street, for occasionally The Child and her friends wanted to rollerblade on a road, wanted to play kickball or catch, wanted to holler out "car!" as The Musician or someone with similar interests would drive—yes, drive!—through.

Outside played The Child.

Many people have a singular thing that defines them. Not all, but many. You may say to me, "But Rye! I have several things that define me! Why, I love to write and I love to paint and I love to cook delicious food," but I might say in return, "My friend, you love to create! You are defined by your creativity."

The Child defined herself by play. She did not merely paint, whether the pictures of which I have already written or the props and backgrounds that adorned the stage, but she played with paint. She was a being of play who, leaning into this identity, had formed as well the vessel with which she navigated the world into that of a child. She was a skunk of five years, or perhaps seven, perhaps ten, and this formation of herself was a means by which she lived wholeheartedly into her identity.

This is the glory of cladistics: that we may become more wholly ourselves. This is what makes us dispersionistas: that we may find joy in this. These simplified dissolution strategies that we have found have less to do with how often we fork, how crowded we may make a room with ourselves, and more to do with how much we love love love the feeling of becoming ourselves while some other us becomes someone else. The Child, The Woman, and I are all of Michelle who was Sasha, we are all some three centuries old, and yet The Child is The Child and The Woman is The Woman and your humble narrator is struggling.

And so The Woman stepped outside where The Child played, turning slow pirouettes, making a clumsy dance along the sidewalk—clumsy in that endearingly childlike way, mind! For that is her role, yes—and at her feet blossomed colored lines in pink orange yellow green blue white chalk, describing the shape of climbing vines, leaves and flowers showing wherever her paws touched the ground. By some trickery of the sim, some trickery wrought by The Oneirotect, her beloved friend and my beloved up-tree, wherever The Child stepped, there blossomed these vines in chalk.

"Hello, Motes," said The Woman.

"Hi," The Child said back. She did not stop in her slow dance, though now, whenever her movements led her to face The Woman, her smile shone bright.

"What are you doing?"

"Just playing. Want to play with me?"

The Woman tilted her head, taking a moment to consider this. "I can try."

"It can be a slower play, if that helps. We do not need to run races or play tag."

She smiled. "I would appreciate that, yes."

"Have you ever seen a five-leaf clover?"

The Woman shook her head.

"Can you imagine one?"

The Woman did so. It was not so hard, she found. She thought of all of the three-leaf clovers that she had seen over the years and decades and centuries—for some of these grew in her very field, and perhaps they flowered, there, as well, those little globes of white—and then added a leaf until she had a four-leaf clover in her mind, and then once more added a leaf.

"Okay, I am imagining it," she said, watching the way The Child moved, the way that she dragged her toes in exaggerated arcs, the way that the vines followed, the way she turned in circles, the way that the vines were tied in knots. "Have you ever seen one?"

The Child shook her head and giggled. "No, I do not think so. That is just the switch."

"The switch?"

"Walk a little bit."

The Woman did so, and was startled to find that her feet, too, described lines in chalk. She laughed. She laughed! My dear, wonderful friends, The Woman laughed! When I spoke with The Child about this day, about the day that The Woman came over to play, The Child agreed with my assessment: seeing The Woman smile, hearing her laugh, they were blessings.

"Come on," The Child said, and The Woman realized she had been fixated on the ground for several seconds and The Child had wandered down the road. "If you walk behind me, I bet we can make them look like a braid."

And so The Woman did, wandering along a few paces behind The Child. They played together in this way, talking quietly as they went. They found that if they walked in a lazy, wavering line, it looked like someone had twisted a rope out of vines of chalk. They found that if The Child orbited the Woman as she walked, the loops that she created were pleasing to behold. They found that, when The Child walked beside The Woman, when they held paws and walked and talked, a pair of parallel railroad tracks blossomed behind them, leaves scattered more sparsely on the two that trailed along after The Woman than those that followed The Child.

The Woman knew already that The Child did not have the answer that she sought, not really, but that was not to say that there was not joy to be found. There was joy in the walk they took. There was joy in the way that they sat on the swings and swayed back and forth. There was joy in watching The Child make little bets with herself and the world around her—"I bet I can make it to the top of the jungle gym in five seconds!" or "I bet I can go down the slide backwards and not die!"—even when she lost those bets—though she did not die that day.

There was, last of all, joy when a piercing whistle broke the quiet of the late afternoon and Motes immediately hopped down from a balance beam and ran up to The Woman. "That was Ma!" This, you see, is what she called My Friend, her down-tree instance who had taken a role not dissimilar from a mother for her. "Dinner is ready. I think Bee–" This, you see, is what she called The Musician, her other guardian and My Friend's partner. "–made meatloaf. Can I give you a hug?"

The Woman smiled, nodded, and sank to a knee so that she could give to The Child the hug which she sought. "Thank you, Motes. Enjoy your dinner. Thank you more than you know."

This day, you see, this day was also not without forward

movement, for The Child said something while climbing a tree that caught The Woman unawares, like the surprise of finding a shiny rock on the ground or perhaps seeing a shape in the clouds. The Child, climbing up a tree with great skill, mentioned in a stream of ceaseless chatter, "One time, Serene turned herself into a tree! She said that she wanted to see what it was like to truly live within one of her sims, you know? She made a bunch of this sim, too! She said she wanted to see what it was like to be a part of something she made. So out there, out on the field out back of the houses, she made herself into this *huge* maple tree! She made it a whole six months like that, then turned back into a fox again. She said it was really boring being so still. She said coming back was like being born, though. That is neat, is it not?"

The Woman wanted to unbecome.

We know this, you and I. We know this because that is the story that I have been telling this whole time, is it not? I have written thousands of words, now, about how she was seeking joy. I wrote of her eating wonderful things, of having sex with her lover and holding hands with her friend, of reading and listening to music, of the conversation she had about creation with me and my beloved up-tree, The Oneirotect, of the mournful prayer she shared with Her Cocladist. I wrote about all of her successes and how each was tainted by an incompleteness, a failure to find the joy she sought, but I have made it so tenuous as to why these two ideas of joy and unbecoming are connected.

The Woman was too much herself, and becoming ever more so always. With each day, each hour, each minute and second, she was becoming ever more herself. She did not just become older—and, dear ones, you remember, of course, that we are *very* old—though she also became that—but she became yet more The Woman than she had been before. My clever readers will remember when I said: I think she would say that she was *too* full, too much, too alive. Those readers will remember when I said: she is too much herself, too human, too embodied within her vessel as it spirals out of control, too stuck in her mind as it twists in on itself. And, yes, those same readers will remember when I said: It is hard to experience peace, hard to experience joy when one is too much oneself, is it not?

Do you see now the connection?

If you sense within The Woman's words and actions a haste to find some joy, some way to unbecome, before some unknown future calamity, I do not think you would be wrong, but neither do I think you would be wholly correct. I think there is a haste within all of us to do what we will before death. Even those of us who live with what we had assumed was functional immortality have found that there is calamity in our lives, for we have now lived through death. No one who uploads even this very day will not remember the calamity that was the Century Attack, the way that a virus had been loosed within Lagrange, within the System in which we dwell, and crashed every single instance. No one who uploads even this very day will not know what terrors we have lived through, the grief of losing one percent of a society 2.3 trillion strong.

I write this in systime 285, in 2409 common era, in 6169 of the Hebrew calendar. If one were to upload as soon as they could, as soon as they turned eighteen, then they would have been nine during the Century Attack, during that one year, one month, and ten days that Lagrange remained offline, all of us functionally immortal rendered functionally dead.

All of us, even those who are uploading today, know that there is haste to do what one will before death.

Oh, it is not so bad as it was at first. Even now, I am finding that I am no longer racing quite so much to spend as much time with my stanza, to get every hug that I can from my beloved up-tree, to eat every good food I can or visit all of the lovely sims out there. I still spend time with my stanza and hug my beloved up-tree and eat good foods and see lovely places, and my beautiful, beautiful readers will certainly recognize the urgency in me writing down all the words I have to say, but it no longer comes with the knife-edge at my throat.

Well.

There is a burning within me, and perhaps it is the burning edge of a knife held to my throat, in order to put all of these words somewhere. Their flow has been unstoppered, and I am helpless before it. They rush at me and all I can do is turn away from the wind and let this flow rush down my arm and out my paw and onto the page—though, my friends, I have now injured my paw too much for this to be literal; there is blood in my fur and under my claws and there are holes in my pads where I punctured them and I still have not had the focus to fork such away and so I write now solely within my head as I pace the quiet rooms of my home.

Time is a story I tell myself. Sentences twine around seconds like tendrils of loveliness or despair or energy or lethargy. Minutes are paragraphs of weal or woe. My hours are scenes that I live out. Days: drabbles. Months: novellas. Years: novels.

But a life? What is a life, anymore? Three centuries and no sign of quitting, and a lifetime seems to have lost meaning. Perhaps someday my life will end, and I will have left behind a finite oeuvre. Perhaps I will simply decide that I have had enough and draw a line across the end of the page and, however many book-shelves of story are left behind shall be all that ever was.

Not yet, though. Not this year, I suspect not this decade, and I hope not even this century.

I have joys to counter all of my sorrows. My head is, yes, in clouds stormy or peaceful, but my feet remain firmly planted on the ground. My arms are full of the love of life. My home makes room for those I see as my family. Our lawns are for picnics and our beds are for dreams.

And so I sit in my office and write my stories. I sit on the couch and dream them up in my head. I cook with my beloved up-tree and watch em and The Child play in the grass while building my ballads after our picnics. I host my joys and languish in my sorrows, and I fall apart into distortion when I overflow. Cuckoo for Cocoa-Puffs, The Oneirotect calls me, and we laugh together.

That is now. That is when I wander the empty rooms of my house and drown in words with tears of ink upon my cheeks and the blood of helplessness still in my paws.

Time is a story I tell myself and this is nothing special. Time is a story *we* tell *ourselves.* Time is a story that Michelle who was Sasha told herself, and her ending was one of—I hope—joy. Time is a story that Qoheleth told himself and his ending was one of—would that it were not—agony. Time is a story that The Woman told herself and her ending was...

Was it? Was hers an ending?

That is her own joy. That is her story. Her story is one of ambiguities and unanswered questions. Her ending is a question mark and a faint smile.

There is a burning, and there is helplessness, but there is no longer *haste,* I mean to say, and I do not think The Woman felt haste. She, like me, felt *compulsion.*

She was compelled to seek a way to unbecome and make room for joy.

×

The Woman wanted to unbecome.

I am doing my best to tell you, dear readers, this story from front to back like any good fairy tale. I am, of course, failing at times to do so like any good author must. Our lives are full of doublings-back and loop-the-loops even when we are bound by time's oh-so-strict arrow, yes? For our lives are circuitous and the progression of the world, as we know, spirals and coils around us.

And so it is that I must once more step back from my notes— and here you must imagine me the type to have notes—and trace my finger up along the timeline of what I have so far told you so that we may sit together and consider why it is that stillness, for The Woman, has so much to do with unbecoming.

We must first of all unlearn the idea that unbecoming is an active process. There may be agency involved—in fact, I think The Woman would insist that there *must* be agency involved, though I think she might hesitate if you were to ask whose agency—but that does not mean that this is a process of undoing-of-self. It is not, as The Woman stated so explicitly, dying, of course, but neither is it coming apart.

The agency, then, comes mostly in the act of choice. I mentioned above or perhaps some pages back that The Woman held onto the thought that stillness lay in choice. I said this because we are so beholden to what we were and what we have become and what we fear we may yet be that we so often lack choice. Perhaps this is an issue faced by all of humanity, but for me and for The Woman and for my beloved up-tree and for all of our clade, it is of the utmost importance, for we are so often and in so many subtle ways unable to make choices ourselves. Oh, I can choose what to wear, perhaps, or what pen to pick up, or when to schedule one of those lovely picnic lunches that the ninth stanza so enjoys, with Praise's music and Warmth's food and Praiseworthy's inscrutable smiles and all of the varied ways in which we love each other.

There is agency, yes, and there is choice and there is a movement toward, for such is the nature of seeking change, but there is also passivity, a moving into passivity, an acceptance of passivity. The Woman, this beautiful woman whose smiles are blessings and whose life is a story—this story! Dear readers, this story!—wished to be still. She wished her unbecoming to be a stillness of her form, perhaps, and her thoughts, to be sure, but also of her very self. She wanted a self locked in joy. She wanted to be as Michelle was in that moment, that final moment, that moment when she looked up to the sun, looked up to our *HaShem*, looked up to The Dreamer, and became a fount of joy, of memory, of thousands of collective years of existence compressed into one self, and she wanted to be in that moment: laid bare and elongated and eternal and forever and unceasing and forever entwined.

She wanted to be defined by joy, not suffering.

x

"I want to unbecome," The Woman told Her Friend.

These two, these two skunks who were women who were both, at their very core, Michelle Hadje who was Sasha, these two sat around a small table not at the coffee shop but out on the field outside of the house where The Woman lived. My readers, most perceptive, will remember that this is where, once every two weeks, unless she was overflowing, unless she was in pain, unless she simply could not bring herself to go, she had an appointment for therapy.

The Woman had requested such, this time, and while it was far from the only time she had done so, the streak of good days, of those days when she felt up to stepping out of the house, out of the sim, out into the city so that they might meet up at a long-familiar coffee shop had been a long one. Her Friend had agreed readily, as ever ey did, but there was within that sensorium message the sense of an eyebrow raised, of a question unasked. And yet, ey said yes, and some ten minutes later arrived, standing out on the grass before the stoop with a mocha in each paw.

Waiting on the first step up from the grass, The Woman bowed and stepped down to greet her friend, and from there, they walked to the table in silence. They lifted down the chairs in silence. They sat down in silence, and sat in silence for some minutes after, until The Woman said, "I want to unbecome."

"So you have mentioned, my dear."

The Woman nodded.

"Have you grown any closer to finding out just what that entails?"

"I have, yes."

Her Friend smiled, raising her paper cup in a toast and tapping it gently to The Woman's own. "Congratulations, End Of Endings. I am pleased to hear that. Is there more that you can tell me?"

"Of course, No Hesitation," The Woman said, sitting up straighter, as though by having her body more in order, her thoughts might be as well—would that this worked, my dear friends! Would that I could be so still and keep my thoughts like ducks: all in a row. Would that my emotions all faced the same direction. Ah, but The Woman continued, "If becoming was the act of going from stillness to movement, then unbecoming might well be the act of going from movement to stillness."

These words apparently caught Her Friend off guard, as ey, too, sat up straighter, furrowing eir brow. I am sure that you can see just how startling such an answer may be! We knew from the start, of course, that talk of unbecoming would be littered with little landmines labeled with such things as 'suicide' or 'self harm' or simply 'the void', of course, but The Woman's words spoke of something more complicated.

"What, then does that stillness look like, to you?" Her Friend asked carefully.

"There are some specifics I have yet to work out, but I can say now that it takes three forms." The Woman held up a paw with three of her fingers raised, and she ticked off each item as she went. "The first form is a spiritual stillness. The second form is a mental stillness. The third form is a physical stillness."

"This sounds a little like meditation."

"There are meditative aspects about it, I would say, but I would not say that it *is* meditation, for it lacks the intent."

"How does it differ, then?"

"Each is an inversion of turmoil. Where there is spiritual unrest, there will be only rest. I do not pray, could not pray, and so this will be an act of becoming okay with that. I can feel RJ in the world, but within that I do not sense any sort of spiritual connection, and so I will become okay with that.

"Where my mind is unsettled, it will be settled. Rather than worrying about my day or about some routine not coming to fruition, I will settle into calm. Instead of thinking myself in circles, I will become a singular point: still and without direction."

"And physically?" Her Friend asked, brow still furrowed. "Will you no longer shift forms?"

The Woman smiled, giving a slight bow. "Yes, No Hesitation. All three of these must work together, yes? If there is turmoil in my thoughts, there will be turmoil in my spirit and I will shift form. If there is turmoil in my spirit, I will think and think and think and shift form. If I become but one form, my mind and my spirit will automatically become that much calmer without that distraction."

Her Friend sighed, and in that sigh was a recognition of unknowing, of ignorance. Ey knew, I think—I think because ey has told me—that ey did not truly understand what it was that The Woman was aiming at. And yet, to ask–! How to ask questions such as what ey wished? There are words and words, and words and words and words that all feel so loaded, yes? They are overburdened with meaning and meaning and meaning. They are too hot, my beloved friends, they are much too hot, and so we must pick them up with tongs and wear thick gloves and perhaps dark glasses over our eyes as the coals glow ruddy- cherry- orange- white- no, blue hot.

And so there was nothing for it.

"End Of Endings," she said most delicately. "I ask this as your friend, but are you safe?"

The Woman, sat in silence for some time, then. They both sat in silence, yes, frozen into a comic panel, those words hanging in the air between them in some invisible speech bubble.

"Yes," she said at last. "Yes, I think I am. There is no death in me. I stand by my words that I do not wish to die, nor do I wish to break apart. I have an idea of what this will look like, and I have an idea of how to approach it, and now all I need is a path from here to there."

Her Friend bowed. "I trust you, my dear. I have no other choice, of course, but I really do trust you. I love you dearly and wish nothing but the best for you."

The Woman smiled and, yes, it was a blessing.

Ah, my dear readers, my dear friends, my lovely little ones who sit criss-cross on carpet squares and the great big ones who wear their hearts on their sleeves, I am unable to do aught else but wax rhapsodic about so lovely a heart as that of The Woman, and while it may sound like I harbor some secret feelings, some hidden affection for her, and while that may indeed be true, for everyone wishes to be blessed by the kindest of smiles, I also feel that I do not have much longer to tell you this story, to finish what I have written from beginning to end, to get to the ending that doubtless you know now is coming, for I am now more words than I am person, I am more sentences than your narrator, and I am more story than I am alive.

I do not have much longer in which I may be able to tell you this story before the ceaseless tangle of words drags me under. I will try. I will try. I will try and try and try, and try and try.

I am very nearly there, too, to the end that you doubtless know is coming. There is only one new face to introduce, one new gently obscured name, and through her, I hope to draw strength, for you have seen already that relying on remembered dialogue makes it easier for me to pin myself to coherency.

×

We are women, much of the clade. There are some men, yes, and many who have exited such limitations as gender offers, but many of us remain women. Woman who are skunks, perhaps, or women who are cats, or women who are shaped some other thing—for is not there also joy in the furry identity with which we fell in love so many centuries ago?—but we are women still. We are so many of us still the short and fat and white and Jewish and dramatic and at-times-ebullient and at-times-depressed women that once Michelle who was Sasha embodied.

I can still look like this! I think we all can. You know as well as I do, dear friends, that our memory is untainted by time, that years and years, and years and years and years may pass, and yet we remember so much with such clarity that it makes me wonder, sometimes, and it makes me tremble. How clearly I remember the day! How clearly I remember the day that, having made it at last to the north north north and west of Yakutsk, my friend Debarre and I sat in a waiting room–

My friends, those of you who uploaded more recently, who uploaded even around the time of Secession must understand just how *complicated* everything was. We uploaded, Debarre and I uploaded as soon as we could afford to. It was so expensive, those days! It was so expensive and I scrimped and saved for almost two years as soon as the procedure was announced and Debarre wiped all his savings and his retirement account and liquidated his stock and even then—*even then!*—we still had to borrow money from...ah, but I am wandering.

Our memory is as perfect and untainted by time as ever it has been since that first day that we uploaded–

My friend Debarre and I gathered every penny, and even then we still had to borrow some few thousand dollars to make the final trip from the central corridor of North America to the very first location of the System, up north north north and west of Yakutsk, where we stayed two nights in a hotel room or perhaps repurposed apartment yellowed to sepia by age, where the kettle was white enameled with a faint floral print around the lid, and yet the bottom of it had been so carbonized over time that it was blacker than black, and may well be the inspiration for The Child's paintings, and there we spent a night and a day and part of a night talking and talking, and talking and talking and talking, asking each other over and over and over who would go first, for the last thing we were told after we were shown to our door, after we were told that we would be locked in for security's sake, after we were told to simply lift the receiver on the ancient telephone if we needed anything beyond water, was that our procedures would not be taking place on the same day, that one of us would have to wait one more day, that one of us would have to sit, aching, locked in the apartment for twenty-four hours longer than the other, that one of us would not hear whether or not the other's procedure was successful and yet would still be committed either way to their own, that we would not know of success or failure until after all was said and done, and could we please simply lift the receiver on the ancient telephone to tell them by midnight...ah, but I am wandering.

What I mean to say is that our memory is perfect, that I can still look like that scared, scared woman—a woman who was sometimes a skunk, yes, and who remembered being at times a panther, but still a woman—who first uploaded within a day of her friend Debarre–

And so we were locked into that room together, that hotel room or perhaps repurposed apartment yellowed to sepia by age, drinking tea after tea after tea because we were too nervous to sleep and not allowed to eat any food until just before the procedure, when we would be offered a hearty breakfast so that we would not upload feeling hungry, to that world that did not yet have food, or at least not satiation. We sat and we drank tea and we held hands and we talked quietly with each other trying to decide who would sit and ache, locked in a hotel room or apartment, and who would sit and ache, locked in some new world of uploaded minds. We sat and we drank tea and we begged and pleaded first for one and then the other, and then we lay down on the two single beds in the dark, facing each other, that first night, and begged and pleaded yet more until, finally, we pulled out the nightstand that sat between them and pushed the beds together so that we could once more hold hands in silence, wondering to ourselves who it was who would be the first, and then, at ten 'til midnight, we lifted the receiver on the ancient telephone...ah, but I am wandering.

Ah, my dear, *dear* readers, you know that I am struggling, I will not apologize any further than I have already. I will focus, and I will tell you about shapes.

What I have meant to tell you, what I have been trying to tell you and failing as waves of words wash over me, is that I remember what it was like to be that shape. I, *too,* can look like Michelle who was Sasha did. I do not choose to do so often—I have not lived so in some decades—but I know that I still can, for I just now tried forking into such a shape. The Woman looked like that perhaps one third of the time, yes?

Many of those within our clade still look like her, to some extent or another, and one of those, one who came to visit me not a month after I met with The Woman, was The Blue Fairy.

The Blue Fairy did not look *precisely* as Michelle who was Sasha did, of course, and very few of us do, except perhaps some of those in the tenth stanza. For, you see, the sixth stanza, the one from which The Blue Fairy originates, found itself focused keenly on feelings of motherhood. This is not, you must understand, restricted to those feelings of giving birth—though perhaps some linger in that sense—nor of having or raising children—though The Blue Fairy is called 'Ma 2.0' by The Child— but it is a general sense, a broad definition that encompasses the feelings of love that dwell within us and how they apply to the whole of the world.

For The Blue Fairy, these feelings of motherhood and motherliness and the love of feeling like a mother were directed towards the System itself, the System as a whole, the System as a marvel of a world into which we are dreamed. She is the System's mother, and it is her baby.

When the System coiled around and began to eat its own tail, when it was attacked, when it was destroyed and reborn, when the fury of a few grew too strong and they wished the lives of all to be ceased, when the Century Attack hit us and so, so many were lost, The Blue Fairy said: "I feel like my baby has stumbled.

The System stumbled and fell, knocked its head, forgotten some of what it knew. I feel like our existence stumbled, as some group or another got so frustrated as to trip it up. When I dump my energy into all of this work, I am doing my best to nurse it back to health."

Do you see, now? Lagrange is her child, and she is its mother.

For some years, for some handful of decades, for nearly a century, she worked as a systech, as one of those who work in service of our world, finding those who have crashed and unwinding their core dumps, finding those who are struggling and helping to bring them to safety to comfort to happiness to the present moment. She stepped from sim to sim, wonder at the world filling her eyes and her mind, and she found the ways in which it could be better, could be so much better, and she brought those to the attention of those outside our world, those phys-side techs working jobs so similar to her own.

One day, however many years ago, definitely more than one hundred but certainly less than two, she grew weary of this last aspect, for when it comes to any relationship between two countries—and do not forget, dear readers, we *long* ago seceded! Seceded from the Sino-Russian Bloc and the Western Federation and the rest of the physical world—there was more bureaucracy than there was forward movement, and The Blue Fairy's baby was wrapped up in tape red and yellow.

And so, she forked. She forked into a new fairy, no longer quite so blue, and together they were all but twins. She promised herself a two-week vacation while her twin took her place, time off to wander sims and drink mochas and fall in love with the world again. Two weeks simply became years, is all, definitely more than one hundred but certainly less than two, and her twin—now with a name of her own—continued on in her stead, and they loved each other for what each had done—The Blue Fairy loved her twin for carrying on in the work, and her twin loved The Blue Fairy for finding ways to love the world.

I do not know why she thought aught else would happen, for Michelle who was Sasha said the same thing, did she not? She said to herself, "Ah, I am so tired, and I feel so broken, and so I will fork the first ten instances of my clade and take a fucking vacation", and she never did return, did she? The Blue Fairy said, "Ah, I am so tired, and so I will fork a new me and take a fucking vacation", and this was the origin of her beloved twin, her beloved twin who carried on in the work, her beloved twin who loved her in turn for finding ways to love the world.

They loved each other, and then, as has been the theme throughout this winding story, the world coiled around and ate itself and a score and a handful of billions of our two-and-change trillion souls did not return, and among them was The Blue Fairy's twin. They loved each other right up until the end, and then The Blue Fairy loved her lost twin alone.

And so here she was, no longer just a cocladist of mine, just a woman who wandered sims and drank mochas and loved the world, but once more a systech, once more a fairy. She was once more The Blue Fairy.

And so here she was, *here,* Standing before my door, my second visitor in a month, bowing to me and greeting me with such kindness as I have ever seen from her, whenever we have had cause to meet—not infrequently, for she was also fond of my beloved up-tree.

"Tell me, Dry Grass, how you have been," I said once we were settled around the table in my house, that dining table which so easily expanded to fit all who would join and yet now was small and intimate.

"Oh, well enough, I suppose. I think I am starting to find my way out of that phase where everything feels new about systech stuff. It was easy enough for me to jump right back in at first, but so much has changed in the intervening years."

"I can imagine, yes."

"It is not all on me, at least. We are all learning the ins and outs of the new tech they have given us while bringing Lagrange back up from the Century Attack. So many crashes after long-diverged forks merged cross-tree out of fun, so many instances of people accidentally messing up their new ACLs and locking themselves out of their own rooms." She laughed, sipped her mocha, and added, "The world feels strange and new."

"It does, at that," I said, smiling. "I do not think I am at risk of either of those, at least. I have little interest in cross-tree merging, beyond providing an instance for Ashes Denote That Fire Was."

"Same, on both counts. I believe they have picked up nearly twenty Odists now. They look...well, they certainly have plenty going on, yes?"

I laughed. "Twenty of us, even if we had never forked, would be, what, six thousand years of memory? And we are not exactly known for never forking, yes? I would say that is plenty."

The Blue Fairy nodded and looked out the window for some time, simply resting her cheek on her fist and her elbow on the table, watching the way the leaves flittered and flickered in the gentle breeze of the day. There is a comfortably jittery quality to such flitting and flickering that reminds me that no one thing in the world is still, and certainly not trees.

Eventually, she replied: "That is actually part of why I came here, Rye."

"Oh?"

"I came to speak with you about End Of Endings."

I sat up straighter. My friends, you will surely understand when I say that The Woman had been on my mind much in the intervening days, in that month between when I last saw her and this lovely afternoon with The Blue Fairy. Her loveliness shined bright in my thoughts, and I still felt blessed—still *feel* blessed!—by each and every one of her smiles and quiet laughs. "Yes, I have spoken with her recently. Warmth and I both have, I mean."

"Yes, she mentioned such to me. She mentioned you two, Motes, Slow Hours, Beholden, No Hesitation, Ever Dream, Rejoice, Farai—a woman with whom she has at times dated—and a few incidental friends she has made in the last month or so. I have been meeting up with each of them to get a better sense of what is happening. You are the last on my list."

I thought this through—and even thinking through it now, I wonder at it. I wonder and I tremble. The Blue Fairy gave me her reason—"I am asking you last of all because I think your experience with stories may help me make better sense of everything," she said when I asked *why me*—and yet even now I linger on this thought that The Woman wove between us all—between all of those that The Blue Fairy mentioned—a gossamer web of connections. She was the strands—perhaps she still remains those strands!—and along those spider-silk-thin lines flow connections built on the blessings she bestowed upon us all. We do not feel stuck, I do not think. We are not bugs in someone absent spider's web. But what are we? Are we the nodes? Are we the sticky radial lines capturing ideas of her, or are we the unsticky spiral that allows us to pick apart our understanding? I tremble. I wonder.

I spoke then at length with The Blue Fairy, hearing all that she had to say, all that I have told you, dear readers, already, and so much more. So, *so* much more! For The Woman had sat with The Blue Fairy for nearly ten hours, expressing all of this and slowly making for her an argument.

Her argument was thus: The Woman knew that there was suffering in her as she was. She knew that she was, in some integral way, defined by her un-joy. She knew that this suffering was bound up in her ongoing process of becoming, of this ever-increasing entropy of the self as time wrought its cruel machinations on her soul.

If, then, her suffering was bound up in increasing entropy, in increasing movement, then perhaps there was joy in stillness. Perhaps that is where her un-suffering lay.

Her argument was to set all movement aside and to follow a dream I have already mentioned. Her dream. My dream. Her argument was that she should become an entity that was still that she may dwell within un-suffering, and that she should spend an eternity thus formed.

"So, what do you think?" The Blue Fairy asked when she presented this argument to me. "I have my own thoughts, but before I share them, I would like to hear from you."

"It sounds...well, it sounds a little fragile, in its conception.

She says that she is not interested in meditating, but she speaks of an essential emptiness, yes?"

The Blue Fairy nodded. "She is not interested in meditating, no."

"Yes. She says that she is uninterested in exploring more paths of greater action. She is not interested in hedonism, and yet her search is one of a pure joy that overrides everything else, yes?"

She nodded once more. "Right."

My friends, I will not lie, there was much frustration in me at the moment. I could feel my tail bristling out and I could feel my hackles raise and I could feel the way my ears were pinning back almost against my will. I think you may well understand, why, too, for this is what I said next: "Okay, and she says that she has no desire to die in her, and yet she is talking about all but disappearing to the world around her, yes? That is what she is saying here! She is saying that she wants to stop being what she is and to become a tree. A tree!"

The Blue Fairy only smiled tiredly to me and replied, "It is as you say."

It took me a few seconds, yes, but I was able to draw calm from her and to settle my nerves. "You think she should go through with this, do you not? Turn into a tree? Die, for all intents and purposes, to the world around her?"

"Yes."

"Unequivocally?"

She shook her head, chuckling. "Oh, not at all. I am quite back-and-forth on this whole thing. At first, I did not agree. She asked me if I would turn her into a tree with little else in the way of explanation and I simply referred her to some groups interested in such things."

"I have heard of those, yes. I have visited Nanbrethil."

"Of course you have," she said, smirking. "But no, she said that she had already read up on some such groups and did not think that this is what she was after. She was after specifically 'unbecoming', and this, she believed, was not the same as the thing that these groups were after. She said, "They are after an experience, and I do not fault them for that, but I am after an existence. They wish to do, I wish to be." When I suggested that perhaps there might be others who are interested in that, she cut me off—very politely, of course!—and said that that may well be, but that she came to me specifically because of our connection."

"Connection?"

"I lost In The Wind, she lost Should We Forget." The Blue Fairy averted her gaze. "I changed because of that loss. I got back into being a systech, yes?"

I sat back in my chair, holding my mug in both paws to draw from the warmth. "Do you think, then, that she is seeking this change because of the loss from the Century Attack? That of Should We Forget?"

"That is what I came to ask you about. I have visited with all of these people, heard all of what they have had to tell me about End Of Endings's last few weeks, and now I want to hear how you would write the end of this story, and how you imagine she would justify it. How *we* might justify it"

Now *this* was a thought, dear readers. This was a thought that danced up along my nape and left a tingle in my scalp, it is a thought that danced down along my arms and gave an inch in my paws that invited the picking up of a pen. It is a thought that has circled around my head like a halo, lighting all that I see, for some years now, for nearly six years! I thought to write this story then, and I thought to write this story after, and I thought to write this story in the intervening years, but something was not quite right, not quite right, not quite right about the time or about myself or about the world around me, and so I did not. I did not write the story perhaps because I was still living in that haste to experience all that I could before our world risked once more coiling around and eating some billions more of us and our lives were turned off like a simple light switch. I did not write the story because I was writing only the small things, that I might spend the rest of my time loving those around me, hugging my beloved up-tree, eating picnics out on the lawn with my stanza, simply *living.* Ah, I am trying to–

Some of you, perhaps some of my newer uploads, or my littler readers who sit criss-cross-applesauce on carpet squares, or maybe some of those who have lived for centuries, might wonder at this. They might wonder: "Rye, it seems to me like The Woman is asking to be absolved of all those except the barest responsibilities of living." They might wonder: "Rye, it seems to me like The Woman is abdicating on life in a way that she can deny is suicide." Perhaps they might wonder: "Rye, The Woman has chosen for herself a next step, a beautiful exploration." And all of them might wonder: "Rye, why is it that you are being asked this in particular? Why is The Blue Fairy not asking for your opinion on whether The Woman should or should not do this thing?"

And I think that, to these musings, I might reply: "My friends, my lovely friends, a beautiful consequence of cladistics is that this is simply not my role. Yes, I had feelings on the thought of The Woman existing within perpetual stillness—of course I did! How then would I be blessed once more by her smile?—and I did indeed tell those to The Blue Fairy, as you shall see, but that is the easy part. The hard part and the valuable thing that I might have to offer is that aspect that I have focused my life around, which is the telling of stories. There are others who might offer predictions for the future, those such as The Poet who live their life in prophecies, but it is my life to write the stories of the now, of the present, of the lives we are living and breathing pinned at the forefront of time's inevitable arrow. The Blue Fairy came to me with all of this research that I might have done myself when it comes to writing a story and asked me to build up a sense of The Woman's life that we may better understand."

And so, I agreed, and The Blue Fairy and I decided that I would sleep on it for one night, and then talked of other things for a few minutes longer before she quit to merge back down, while I bathed in this research already done, and told within myself a story.

"There are two ways that I see this ending," I said when we met the next morning. "The first is that you and her work together to help her accomplish her goal. She becomes still in the form of a tree parked in a field–"

"She has requested that she be...uh, planted, I guess, in the sidewalk in front of her favorite coffee shop." She smiled, sheepish, and said, "Sorry, I did not mean to interrupt."

"No, no, that is quite alright. It is sweet, actually, that she found something meaningful like that. But yes, one ending is that she does as she says and that she finds her happiness there, but we are all left with complicated feelings. We will all have lost her, in a way, yes? For, though she has said that she is not aiming to *die,* she will have *effectively* died to us, yes? We will have to process her loss.

"The other ending is that we help her try to find happiness that does not involve another loss within our clade. In this she may find herself confronted with frustration, not just at the denial of her request, but at the fact that, if there does remain some joy that is not stillness, she may encounter more pain in the process of getting there."

She frowned, lingering in silence, and then nodded. "And I worry that that, too, will be uncomfortable for us. We will see her still among us, but will we see her happy? If she is miserable, I do not think I would like that, either."

"Yes. When we spoke yesterday, I was quite against the idea. I know that, if she does continue living, if she does not quit, she can always come back to us, but it still came with a sense of wanting to do everything I could to prevent that." I sighed—I remember that well, I sighed as though I was breathing out my complicated feelings in a way that speaking them would not quite do justice—and continued. "And yet now, having done as you suggested. I feel perhaps more the opposite. If she is, as she has suggested via her various conversations, as Rejoice has suggested, suffering, then who are we to suggest she linger there? Even if it is a kind of suffering that we do not understand, it would be rather cruel of us, would it not? And yet is life not hard? And yet decisions ought to be respected, yes?" I laughed and waggled my paw back and forth. "This is difficult, and that, in and of itself, is a good story."

The Blue Fairy groaned and covered her face in her hands. "Fuck. Rye, why is this so hard? Why did she ask me?"

"Because you are a good person. She respects you, yes? And you are a cocladist. You *are* her, in a way," I said, squeezing her upper arm kindly. "She is looking to someone she respects and someone she *is* to either give her blessing by helping, or to talk her out of it. The decision is not whether or not *she* should, but whether or not *we* should. It is not a judgment on her, if it is a judgment at all, but it is a judgment on us."

I, dear readers, dear, *dear* friends, I am trying to believe this. I am trying to live into this. I am trying to feel that I have been judged for making that decision, the decision that I did, the decision to let go—for I am sure that you see now just where this is going; have I not written so much in the past tense?—and been judged worthy. I hope that, if God exists, that They will smile and brush my mane out of my eyes and rest Their paw—for am I not made in Their image? Am I not *b'tzelem Elohim?*—and say to me, "It is okay, Rye. To let go is difficult, but it is okay. Sometimes one must let go."

But here is the point where my mind was made up, and I will admit to being somewhat ashamed that it was something so simple as this, but I am a simple skunk. One might call me a one-dimensional person and not be wrong. It makes me wonder and it makes me tremble, but this is the point in the story where I made that decision.

"I do not think we would ever know, is all. You are right in that she has said that this is not a death, but we would never know. The reason she came to me is not necessarily to help her turn into a tree—though I will also help her with that—but to modify her record in the perisystem clade listing to be grayed out."

I sat up straighter, hearing this. How intriguing! "As in when one has locked down their visibility?"

"Yes. She requested an exception that, whether or not she quits, her entry remain in some in-between state so that we will never know."

"Has she said why?"

She snorted, raising her face from her hands. "She said that each of us will have to make up our own reason. It was all very Odist."

"It really is," I said, chuckling. Readers, it is so much easier to write like this, to tell of concrete things. I am trying not to rush, as I do not have much time left, I think but– ah, I am interrupting myself. I chuckled and said, "It really is. Did you mention this to the others?"

"I did. Reactions were mixed. Farai cried quite hard. No Hesitation was left in a whirlwind of doubts. Slow Hours agreed immediately that we grant her this change."

"That is very Slow Hours of her."

The Blue Fairy laughed. "I suppose it is."

I struggled for a minute, and it was not for want of words, for I knew the words I needed, but it was for want of courage. I did not know how to say this to her without sounding cruel, perhaps, or uncaring, or self-centered, but I could not be anything other than honest in that moment, not for something so important as this.

"I want that, too," I said.

"Pardon?"

"I want that for her. I want that she be able tell this story for herself. That is my decision."

Her shoulders slumped, and she looked at me with tired eyes, searching eyes. "What is your reason for her request of an exception, then?"

"She is keeping her last bit of agency for herself," I said—slowly, for I was not so rehearsed with these words, and I have a habit of rehearsing much of what I say. "She is saying, "This final decision is mine. You may decide whether or not to help me, but if you do, I will make the final decision." She tells the end of her story alone, and we will have to tell ours for ourselves."

We spent some minutes then in silence—a comfortable silence, friends; I did not feel like we were waiting for the other to speak—simply drinking our mochas and looking out the window together.

At last, The Blue Fairy smiled to me. "Alright. I will do as she has asked. It kills me, Rye. It hurts, but I will do as she has asked."

×

I am struggling and I am crying and I am pacing around my empty house and I am trembling and I am struggling and I am crying and my paws are bleeding from where my claws have pierced my pads and I am having a hard time holding myself down to one set of thoughts to one set of words to one language to the present moment to the living world and I am looking up and within and without and around and hunting for our superlative friend who is The Dreamer who dreams us all and I am struggling and I am crying and I am doing my best not to step away to that sim to that coffeeshop to that tree where I may throw myself at its roots and wrap my arms around its trunk and press my cheek against its coarse bark and weep and weep and weep and weep and weep and weep and weep and weep and weep and weep and weep and weep and weep and weep and–

My friends, my beautiful beloved readers, I am lost. I am all but lost. I have enough in me to tell you of what happened, but only just, and then I will no longer be able to continue, for that was the last conversation we had. That is the last concrete thing that I have to write. There are no other words that I can tell you except for these:

*"It is done."*

The Blue Fairy met The Woman at the foot of the steps of the house, that Gothic house on the field of grass and dandelions and perhaps clover. She stood, this wonderful and sad and amazing fairy at the base of the steps of the house and looked up to the door as The Woman stepped forth. With each step, The Woman changed. Every time her foot or paw hit the ground, she became a new thing. She was now The Woman who was The Human and she was now The Woman who was The Panther and she was now The Woman who was The Skunk, and always—*always* always always in all ways always—she was smiling and her smile was a blessing upon the whole of the world. Upon the house, upon the field of grass and dandelions and perhaps clover, upon The Blue Fairy upon, when she turned around, the remainder of her stanza who all stepped out onto the porch to watch her go.

There, The Blue Fairy bowed. She bowed and held out her

hand and let The Woman rest her hand her paw her paw her hand her paw her paw her hand within it to let herself be guided down to the field like some princess greeted by some royal courtier or perhaps a prince from a far away kingdom. There, The Blue Fairy basked in this blessing of a smile from The Woman, her cocladist from far, far across the clade, and led her gently from the field and to the city.

My friends, my dear, *dear* friends, there was no door for her to brush her fingers against, no imagined *mezuzah* that she might touch for some final blessing, and—at last at last for once at last—neither was there a sense of ritual nipping at her heels, following along like some eager puppy. There was no ritual, for she knew now that she created her *own* blessings she created her *own* peace she created her *own* future.

There was no door.

There was no door.

Oh Lord oh Dreamer oh AwDae there was no door.

There was no door, no imagined *mezuzah,* as they stepped through to the city and landed in the alleyway in which The Woman usually arrived. They, then, were briefly alone. They were alone in the cool shade of the buildings and the crispness of the air and the staticky sound of the fallen leaves skittering around their feet and feet and paws and paws and feet and paws and feet and paws and paws and–

They walked lightly and in silence as they stepped along the sidewalk and boarded the trolley to ride three stops, three stops, three stops to the coffee shop that The Woman and Her Friend always loved, and there was no one there—not a request but a felicity a chance a happenstance that befell them, that they stand there at the entrance to the coffee shop that The Woman and Her Friend always loved alone and surrounded by the quiet sounds of the breeze that wafted between the buildings and past doors and against skin against fur against fur against skin against skin against skin against fur against skin against–

The Woman and The Blue Fairy stood before the coffeeshop on the sidewalk where there was a new thing, where there was a square cut into the paving stones on the sidewalk two meters on a side and a grate of steel or iron set into it with a sunburst pattern and, in the center, a circle of good, clean soil.

There, The Woman turned a slow circle and smiled one final blessing on the world and faced at last The Blue Fairy, who would be the last person to be so blessed, and The Blue Fairy guided The Woman The Skunk The Panther The Woman The Woman The Woman The Woman down to her knees and knelt with her and reached up and brushed her hair her mane her forehead her hair her mane her forehead, and leaned in to place a gentle kiss atop her head, and then The Woman nodded, and then The Blue Fairy stood and, crying, signaled to the System The Dreamer our superlative friend our personal *HaShem* that all was as it should be and that all should proceed as it ought and then, there, at last, finally, without further action, she watched.

The Woman, as she dreamed, as I have always dreamed since and dreamed before and perhaps all of us dream at some point or another, dug her fingers down into the soil. Down and down and down she pushed, and as she did, she felt her fingers lengthen, stretching and twisting, seeking nutrients and water, seeking final—final!—purchase. They twisted and stretched down as roots and spiraling up her arms was a texture like bark and the bones of her neck and back elongated and her eyes sought *HaShem* or The Dreamer or some greater void and her hair greened to that of leaves and drank thirstily of the sunlight.

She dreamed of words like leaves and sentences like branches and stories like trunks, standing solid, with premises like roots dug into logic like earth and drinking of emotions like water. There was the tree, yes, for there was the green of the words and the brown of the story and the deep darkness of logic and emotion.

And above was the sun which was also AwDae who was RJ, The Dreamer who dreams us all.

Finally—finally!—with one orgasmic flush of joy, The Woman became The Tree, and there was a joy everlasting in such stillness.

There, The Blue Fairy stood for for an hour or more, simply crying, now standing before the tree, now sitting at its base, now pacing a long circle around it, and always she cried, and she watered the thirsty roots of The Tree which once was The Woman with her tears and the passers-by looked on with curiosity or studiously ignored her or perhaps offered words of condolences, but all—all all all all *all*—looked on with wonder at this brand new thing, this new occurrence, this new beauty of a tree, a catalpa that would one day bloom white flowers and leave behind forgotten pods of seeds that rattled joyously against the ground.

And then, when her tears were gone and the roots of The Tree had slaked their thirst, The Blue Fairy sent us all a simple message, three simple words, one by one by one by one by one by one by one by one by one by one by one she told us:

*"It is done."*

We may never more be blessed.

We may never more be blessed.

*Baruch atah Adonai Eloneinu melech ha'olam dayan ha'emet* we may never more be blessed.

I may never more melt beneath her smile, may never again cry before her. What will become of me?

The Child may never more play with her, wandering around the streets with lines of chalk following their feet, making little bets with themselves. What will become of her?

Her Cocladist will never wonder whether there is aught else in life but suffering while The Woman sits nearby. What will become of her?

The Oneirotect may never more share stories of Should We Forget, nor bring her small treats, small gifts. What will become of it?

Where before The Woman and Her Lover, as the poet says, shared their oranges and limes, where they gave their kisses, where they lay on the grass and beach, now the woman lays underground and they share nothing, giving silence for silence. What will become of her?

What of Her Friend? What of that beautiful soul? What of em? What of the one who goes now to the coffee shop every day and drinks her mocha by the base of The Tree, eir tail curled over eir paws, and speaks aloud to one who is lost to em? What will become of em?

The Poet! The Musician! The aesthetician and that kindly restaurateur who petted her head while she sobbed at the remembered pain of spice and the Dreamer above! What will become of *all* of them?

And all of this makes me wonder and makes me tremble.

It makes me tremble and it makes my fur stand on end and my paws shake and my pen skitter anxiously across the page like those leaves that danced before the feet of The Woman I told you about so, so long ago, perhaps like those leaves that skitter within the city, that unreal city, that city full of dreams, where the souls of the lost in broad daylight cling to passers-by.

Oh! And oh! The wonder of it all! She, then, like so many leaves and the white petals of flowers and the dry brown pods of seeds fell secretly! She fell and fell and fell and we fell and fell and fell and fell and fell until falling was all we knew and within that fall we found some new kernel of truth but how hot that kernel was! It burned within our palm as we held it to our chest and for each of us it burned so, so hot and so, so differently that there she was, too much herself and here I am, too much myself, and the words come so fast and so thick that I am blinded! Ink in my eyes! Scrabbling for any known thing! I press upon this and that with shaking fingertips to try and find something that is not yet more words, but that is all there is, because this is it, my friends, the kernel of truth that we found. The truth we now know is that we are falling still! That unfalling ones are trapped within that last falling! We fell into overflow and never really ever came back. We may slow down, we may catch a branch of The Tree and be able to hold there for a little while, panting, struggling to catch our breath, until fire burns through our shoulders and we cannot hold any longer and we are forced to let go once more and fall and fall and fall just like I am falling and falling and falling and falling and falling and–

And The Woman? This is what makes me wonder and makes me tremble: what of her? Is she alive still? Or did she quit and are we left not with The Tree that is her but simply a tree? Simply that which drinks thirstily from this dream of a ground. Is that her or is it a dream of dumb matter? If she is still there, if she is still alive, if she is still The Tree, then is she still at last? Is she merely herself at last? Has she landed at last upon the ground and sat up, dazed, and looked about her new life and said, "Oh! Oh, I do believe this is some plentiful enough for me"?

Because if that is so, what of us? My little readers may be rubbing the tears from their eyes or tilting their heads in confusion as I wonder at them: what of us? If that really *is* her, if she really *is* The Tree, and if she really *is* finally—finally!—still, then what does that mean for me, who cries ink down into her fur—a skunk! Is it really any wonder that black fur suits me so? What does that mean for my clade? For Her Friend, who struggles and strives to reclaim that which has failed and turn it into some bijou and yet who, when ey falls, feels that all the work ey has done is not just for naught, but has hurt those who ey sought to help?

My own Friend, who will most certainly read this and reach out to me to see if I am okay, she has said that she wonders at times whether we are all doomed to die. She was with me— with all of us there on the field—as I watched my root instance look up to the sky, breathe in a million billion trillion years and then quit, and so now she wonders at times whether we are all doomed to do as she did, to look up to the sky, breathe in every year of our lives and the lives of all of our instances, and quit. If that is all that lays before us, what does that mean for us? If all that lies before every Odist and every hidden, forbidden self that we have spun out into the world is some forever death, then what does that mean for this time-bound now?

Is death within us? Perhaps. Is suicide within us? Perhaps.

Was this death? Was what The Woman did in seeking and finding her eternal stillness suicide? Perhaps! Perhaps perhaps perhaps perhaps my friends perhaps–

My little readers who are rubbing the tears from their eyes, do not fret! Do not fret. Do not fret. Do not fret. These are the questions that are part of life. Do not fret that you, too, may someday ask yourself this: is death within me? Am I born to die? Perhaps you will lose a friend to despair, as did so many after the world's heart skipped a beat and billions fell into oblivion. Perhaps you, yourself will despair and then come back up to feel the sun on your cheeks in some prosaic sim and wonder: am I born to die?

When, as now, I am blinded by ink that flows down my cheeks and stains my fur and my clothes and my paws and my paper and my pen and my desk or when, as now, I overflow and graphomania catches me up by the throat and bids me with un-bitter sweetness to set the nib of my pen in the ink well, then touch it to the page, and then simply dance, that is when I am forced to wonder, when I am pressed up against that overhot kernel of truth: is death within me? Is suicide within me? And am I born to die?

What will become of me?

Friends, I do not know, I do not know. Most beloved, all I can do is lock the door and make sure my mug of mocha will not empty and pick up my pen and put it to the paper and brush my cheek fondly against my graphomania's wrist and listen to its cloying words and simply dance. Do I need help? Should I seek out No Hesitation? Should I ask My Friend? Should I ask you, gentle readers? What will happen if I do? What will happen if I do not? What will become of me?

I am full of wonder and I am full of terror and I am trembling and I am asking myself you The Woman Her Friend My Friend my graphomania my pen my paper my dear, *dear* readers: what will become of me, and am I born to die? And am I born to die? And am I born to die? What will become of me? And am I born to die? What will become of me? What will become of me? What will become of me? What will become of me? And am I born to die? And am I born to die? What will become of me?  And am I born to die? And am I born to die? And am I born to die? And am I born to die? And am I born to die? And am I born to die? And am I born to die? And am I born to die? And am I born to die? And am I born to die? And am I born to die? And am I born to die? And am I born to die? And am I born to die? And am I born to die? And am I born to die? And am I born to die? And am I born to die? And am I born to die? And am I born to die? And am I born to die? And am I born to die? And am I born to die? And am I born to die? And am I born to die? And am I born to die? And am I born to die?
And am I born to die?

And am I born to die?                                        And am I born to die? And am I born to die? And am I born to die? What will become of me? And am I born to die? And am I born to die? And am I born to die? And am I born to die? And am I born

Idumea

to die? And am I born to die? What will become of me? And
am I born to die? And am I born to die?


And am I born to die?
And am I born to die? And am I born


What will become of me?
to die? And am I born to die? What will become of me? What
will become of me? And am I born to die? And am I born to die?
What will become of me? And am I born to die? And am I born to
die? And am I born to die? And am I born to die? And am I born


to   die?


What will become of me?
What will become of me? What will become of me? And am I
born to die? What will become of me? And am I born to die?


What will become of me? What will
become of me? What will become of me? And am I born to die?
And am I born to die? And am I born to die? And am I born
to die? And am I born to die? And am I born to die? And am I


194

born to die?                              What will become of me?


And am I born to die?
                 And am I born to die? What will become




And am I born to die?

                              What will become of me?



of me?                                        And am



And am I born to die?

Idumea

                                                          And am I born to die?




I born to die? What will become of me?




What  will  become  of  me?                              And
am  I  born  to  die?                        And  am  I  born  to


                    And am I born to die?
die?  And am  I  born  to  die?  And  am  I  born  to  die?  And  am
I  born  to  die?                             What  will  become


What will become of me?
    of  me?  What  will  become  of  me?  And  am  I  born  to  die?
            And am I born to die?




                          What will become of me? What will be-

And am I b

come  of  me?

And am I born to die?

What    will    become    of    me?

What will become of me?
What    will    become    of    me?    And    am    I    born    to    die?
What will become of me?

And  am  I

Idumea

born to die?                              And am I born to die? And am

And am I born to die?
                And am I born to die?

I born to die?

                                    What will become of me?
What    will    become    of    me?

Madison Rye Progress

And am I born to die

And  am  I  born  to  die?                    And  am

I  born  to  die?          And am I born to die?    What  will  become

of    me?

What will become of me?    And am I born to die?

What   will   become   of   me?
And  am  I  born  to  die?And am I born to die?    And  am
I  born  to  die?                    What  will  be-

And am I born to die?

199

Idumea

And am I born to die?

come  of  me?                    What  will  become
                                 And am I born to die?

of me?  What  will  become  of  me?
        What will become of me?

What will become of me?

What will become of me?

orn to die?

200

What will bec

What will become of me?
**What     will     become     of     me?**




And am I born to die?

What will become of me?

What will beco

ome of me?

And

What will become of me?

Idumea

am I born to die?                                     And am I born to


                        What will become of me?
die?


And am I born to die?

✕

# Afterword

# Appendix I — Notes

How do I explain such pages of notes? How do I tell you, beloved readers, that, the more I write, the more feverish my pace, the greater the pull of my graphomania upon my wrist, the more words flow through me *period*? Words that are my own. Words that are nonsense. Words that are, yes, the words of others. It yanks and tugs on my wrist, its other hand—paw?—lingering so sweetly on my neck, drawing lazy fingers across as though to bleed me dry of ink, and from out of me spills my words and also the words that have ever made me what I am.

Here, then, are the references as I remember them. I will apologize no further.


**Page 1**  *But you are eternity and you are the mirror.*

From *The Prophet.*

I had originally intended to use the lyrics from the hymn titled "Idumea", which is included in the next appendix, but—ah! For some reason, it did not fit. I could not tell you why, dear reader. Perhaps it was the strong Christian nature of the text after a certain point, which fit strangely for the Odists, notably Jewish as they are. It, after all, is what spurred the language at the end of my...we shall call it a little meltdown at the end, there, yes?

Perhaps it was that, as the story filled out within the middle, it just did not fit. I, Rye, suffered, perhaps. I wailed, "What will become of me?" I am the one who was overcome by overflow. I promise you, my friends, I *promise* you, however, that this is not my story. The judgment is upon my head for what I have done, but it is not my story. This story belongs to The Woman.

No. Instead, I chose the words of Almustafa, the chosen and the beloved. The Woman was life and she was the veil. We are eternity and the System is the mirror.


**Page 5**   *Once upon a time there was–*

Cf. Carlo Collodi:

> Once upon a time there was–
>
> "A king?" my little readers will immediately say.
>
> No, children, you are mistaken. Once upon a time there was a piece of wood. It was not fine wood, but a simple piece of wood from the wood yard,—the kind we put in the stoves and fireplaces so as to make a fire and heat the rooms.
>
> I do not know how it happened, but one beautiful day a certain old woodcutter found a piece of this kind of wood in his shop. The name of the old man was Antonio, but everybody called him Mas-

ter Cherry on account of the point of his nose, which was always shiny and purplish, just like a ripe cherry...

When first I began to write, back when some saner me put pen to paper, I had intended to write the story of Pinocchio in reverse. "Ah!" I thought. "Perhaps I can very heavy-handed with it, too. Should the main character be named Occhioni P.? Will they try turning themselves into a literal puppet? Will they design sims to include the big fish? Perhaps they will find their Geppetto— G. from Oteppe, Belgium—who unmakes them, and then a blue fairy, a sympathetic systech, kicks them into quitting. Will I tell it as a fairy tale?"

We see how well I have stuck to that plan, yes?

I spoke of this with writer friends, and one of them, the ever delightful Seras of the CERES clade, quipped that this sounded just like the escape from samsara, the cycle of suffering, and I was, as the saying goes, off to the races.

Now here I am, once more coming down from my overflow, once more feeling somewhat grounded, the world around once more made of things which are not yet more words, and I have to contend with the reality that this remains, for the most part, a funny little note, and that this story no longer quite reads as that real-boy-to-inanimate-tree pipeline, tired trope that I am sure it is.

Instead, I must hope that The Woman has indeed escaped such a cycle, and I must hope that those along her way were in some roundabout way akin to the bodhisattvas in her life.

**Page 26**  *[...] am I a falcon, a storm, or a great song?*

From Rainer Maria Rilke:


Ich lebe mein Leben in wachsenden Ringen,
die sich über die Dinge ziehn.
Ich werde den letzten vielleicht nicht vollbringen,
aber versuchen will ich ihn.

Ich kreise um Gott, um den uralten Turm,
und ich kreise jahrtausendelang;
und ich weiß noch nicht: bin ich ein Falke, ein Sturm
oder ein großer Gesang.


×


I live my life in ever-widening circles
that stretch themselves out over the world.
I may not complete this last one
but I will give myself to it.

I circle around God, around the primordial tower.
and I circle for thousands of years
and I still don't know: am I a falcon,
a storm, or a great song?

**Page 26**    [...] *dance unblushing* [...]

Cf. Darius Halley:

> We turn to dust
> Get swept away
> To make room for
> Empty nothing
> Amble through the
> Air and find a
> Ray of light and
> Dance unblushing

**Page 30**    *Where is it that my joy has gone?*

Cf. Dan Simmons:

> Then, on a cool morning with my sleeping room rocking slightly in the upper branches of my tree on the Templar world, I awoke to a gray sky and the realization that my muse had fled.
>
> It had been five years since I had written any poetry. The *Cantos* lay open in the Deneb Drei tower, only a few pages finished beyond what had been published. I had been using thought processors to write my novels and one of these activated as I entered the study. SHIT, it printed out, WHAT DID I DO WITH MY MUSE?

The loss of the intangible stings the most.

**Pages 62, 63, and 189**   *[...] as the poet says, shared [...]*

Cf. Octavio Paz:

Tendidos en la yerba
una muchacha y un muchacho.
Comen naranjas, cambian besos
como las olas cambian sus espumas.

Tendidos en la playa
una muchacha y un muchacho.
Comen limones, cambian beso
como las nubes cambian espumas.

Tendidos bajo tierra
una muchacha y un muchacho.
No dicen nada, no se besan,
cambian silencio por silencio.

×

Lying in the grass
a girl and a boy.
Eating oranges, exchanging kisses
like the waves exchanging their foam.

Lying on the beach
a girl and a boy.
Eating limes, exchanging kisses
like the clouds exchanging foam.

Lying underground
a girl and a boy.
Saying nothing, nor kissing
exchanging silence for silence.

**Page 63**   [...] *a sutle twisting, a stirring, a clockwise motion* [...]

Cf. Simmons:

> They lay next to each other. The dead man's armor was cold against Kassad's left arm, her thigh warm against his right leg. The sunlight was a benediction. Hidden colors rose to the surface of things. Kassad turned his head and gazed at her as she rested her head on his shoulder. Her cheeks glowed with flush and autumn light and her hair lay like copper threads along the flesh of his arm. She curved her leg over his thigh and Kassad felt the clockwise stirring of renewed passion. The sun was warm on his face. He closed his eyes.

The tone, here, is quite different, but it is notable that 'clockwise' would so catch my attention to lodge itself in my mind, when it comes to the topic of sexuality. Perhaps arousal is an unwinding, then, and orgasm the *ding!* when the timer hits zero, and that is why we say 'pent up'.

Perhaps it is simply the nerves I feel about so blatantly describing a sexual act within a supposed fairy tale that leads to a twisting in my own stomach.

I do not know, my friends.

**Page 64**   [...] *there was a spot between joy and fear, a place of too much meaning* [...]

Cf. Slow Hours:

> Inter ĝuo kaj timo
> Estas loko de tro da signifo.
> Apud kompreno, ekster saĝo,
> Tamen ĝi tutampleksas.
> Mi kompareble malgrandas
> Kaj ĝi tro granda estas.
> Nekomprenebla
> Nekontestebla,
> Senmova kaj ĉiam ŝanĝiĝema.

×

> Between joy and fear
> Is a place of too much meaning.
> Next to understanding, outside wisdom,
> It nonetheless expands.
> I am so small beside it
> and it is too big.
> Incomprehensible,
> Incontestible,
> Unmoving and always changing.

**Page 64**   [...] *the orange and blue of love and anxiety* [...]

When one writes of that which is alien in the context of morality, one might say that it escapes even the concepts of black, white, and gray, and instead lies on the axis of blue and orange. Blue-orange morality is that which is so far removed from our on conceptions of good and evil that one whose morals fall along such a spectrum may escape definition of 'good' or 'evil' at all, and so too do they evade 'order' and 'chaos'.

Here, then, may well be your narrator's own complex engagement with romance and sensuality and sexuality peeking through. Here, then, may be a glimpse into the mind of someone who just does not quite get it. It is lovely. I know this. I *know* this, and yet anticipation and anxiety are not black and white to me, they are blue and orange.

The writer, as ever, is a character in their own works, no matter the role they actually play.

**Page 67**  [...] *and she knew that Her Lover would be by her side for some time to come if she let her—and she would let her—and that, too, was a joy.*
Cf. Echo:

> She is to me a cherished thing,
> A queen to a throne, with the wit to reign regent.
> So, to say that she is mine is indeed a crime.
> But if she has asked me to so infringe —
> And she has asked me to so infringe —
> Then mine she shall be
> For she has me woven around her finger
> As she is all the way around mine.

**Page 70**  *[…] and I do not believe she merged cross-tree with anyone except perhaps Ashes Denote That Fire Was, who is building in themself a gestalt of the clade as best they can.*

From Emily Dickinson:

> Ashes denote that Fire was —
> Revere the Grayest Pile
> For the Departed Creature's sake
> That hovered there awhile —
>
> Fire exists the first in light
> And then consolidates
> Only the Chemist can disclose
> Into what Carbonates.

We have always borne an obsession with Emily Dickinson. For years and years, and years and years and years she has lived within us, a remnant of some stage play we performed with our superlative friend, centuries back now.

Is it so surprising, then, that after cross-tree merging had been introduced as an option for us, that the one who would seek to collect within themself the entirety of the Ode clade—those who remain, dear readers!—would take for a name a line of Dickinson? We will be ever ourselves.

**Page 86**  *It was a land of long, rolling hills and yet longer flat basins that always drank most thirstily from the seasonal storms that did their best to thrash the Earth below.*

Cf. Dwale:

The seasonal storms have poured upon the grassy
    flat,
The leafless stalks abound like thirsty mouths.
Puddles form and soon are swarmed with little fish,
And all the arid life has fled despair.

I will admit, my friends, that I had considered penning in the rest of this poem of Dwale's, for it is replete with references joyful and otherwise—"Within her womb there grows a golden bloom": you can see the association with dandelions, yes? Those flowers we are helplessly taken with?—but it is raw, far too raw, to be thinking about the death of winter and the growth implicit in spring when this story I have told ends as it does.

And I am raw, far too raw, to tell it.

**Page 88**   I have written extensively on these hyper-black shapes that The Child paints and more about her besides in *Motes Played*. A little book for little skunks, yes? For she deserves her story told—and just so! Just like this! A tale written in a style befitting her—as much as does The Woman.

**Page 93**   *Miss Michelle Hadje, five foot four.*

Cf. John Keats:

I do think better of womankind than to suppose they
care whether Mister John Keats five feet high likes
them or not.

**Page 95**   On The Oneirotect's pronouns

The Oneirotect uses for itself several pronouns—though the set you see here in this text are 'she', 'they', 'ey', and 'it'—which serves as a reflection both of its critter nature and the fluidity of eir engagement with gender- no, with the slipperiness of identity as a whole. This is the role of language with identity: to be a poor reflection through some imperfect mirror, a version of the self seen through some glass, darkly.

You will note the same is also true of The Dog, who, yes, is prone to a critter nature, but who also sometimes views himself as 'it' and sometimes itself as 'him'. For better or worse the identity of animals, of 'low beasts', is entwined with that of *things,* and for some, that is a joy.


**Page 98**   *It is* enjoyable, *and often it is* loved, *but it is not really* beloved.

Cf. David Rakoff:

> Should you happen to be possessed of a certain verbal acuity coupled with a relentless, hair-trigger humor and surface cheer spackling over a chronic melancholia and loneliness—a grotesquely caricatured version of your deepest self, which you trot out at the slightest provocation to endearing and glib comic effect, thus rendering you the kind of fellow who is beloved by all yet loved by none, all of it to distract, however fleetingly, from the cold and dead-faced truth that with each passing

year you face the unavoidable certainty of a solitary future in which you will perish one day while vainly attempting the Heimlich maneuver on yourself over the back of a kitchen chair—then this confirmation that you have triumphed again and managed to gull yet another mark, except this time it was the one person you'd hoped might be immune to your ever-creakier, puddle-shallow, sideshow-barker variation on adorable, even though you'd been launching this campaign weekly with a single-minded concentration from day one—well, it conjures up feelings that are best described as mixed, to say the least.

The distinction between a thing that is *loved* and a thing that is *beloved* is a type of subtlety that we seem to enjoy dwelling within rather a lot. The Instance Artist has spoken of an anxiety that it might be the type of person who is "beloved by all yet loved by none," given how difficult it felt for it to let anyone get truly close to it. The Oneirotect describes food the other way around, however: ey fears that its food may be merely loved, rather than so much more broadly beloved.

One must never ask an author their desires on where their work ought lie on the loved-beloved scale.

**Page 106**   [...] *all the world's a horror.*

Cf. Shakespeare

> All the world's a stage,
> And all the men and women merely players;
> They have their exits and their entrances [...]

**Page 106**   [...] *through a glass, darkly.*

Cf. 1 Cor 13:12-13 (KJV)

> $^{12}$ For now we see through a glass, darkly; but then face to face: now I know in part; but then shall I know even as also I am known. $^{13}$ And now abideth faith, hope, charity, these three; but the greatest of these is charity.

What a strange man Paul who was Saul of Tarsus was! We, the Ode clade, are Jews by inheritance, if not by belief, and yet even we cannot escape the cultural Christianity that so pervaded society phys-side when still we lived there.

And it is not without beauty, yes? For this passage is beautiful, and so too is more of this chapter:

> $^4$ Love *[as recent versions translate the 'charity' above. —Rye]* is patient; love is kind; love is not envious or boastful or arrogant $^5$ or rude. It does not insist on its own way; it is not irritable; it keeps no record of wrongs; $^6$ it does not rejoice in wrongdoing but rejoices in the truth. $^7$ It bears all things, believes all things, hopes all things, endures all things.

> $^8$ Love never ends. But as for prophecies, they will come to an end; as for tongues, they will cease; as for knowledge, it will come to an end. $^9$ For we know only in part, and we prophesy only in part, $^{10}$ but when the complete comes, the partial will come to an end.

Just as it is not without its terror, yes? For verse 11 was used against The Child in a cutting letter from Hammered Silver, first line of the sixth stanza, from the NRSVUE translation used above:

> [11] When I was a child, I spoke like a child, I thought like a child, I reasoned like a child. When I became an adult, I put an end to childish ways.

Such bitterness! Words as a weapon! I write below of how we loathe our connections, and here was a moment of that loathing, for I remember well the pain that we all felt at that cruelty, but this is not that story, and so I will linger on the ideas of glasses darkly.

**Page 106**   *The Sightwright suffered as I do, as The Oneirotect does, and perhaps even as The Woman did.*

Cf. John Winthrop

> We must delight in each other; make others' conditions our own; rejoice together, mourn together, labor and suffer together, always having before our eyes our commission and community in the work, as members of the same body.
>
> [...]
>
> All the parts of this body being thus united are made so contiguous in a special relation as they must needs partake of each other's strength and infirmity, joy and sorrow, weal and woe. (1 Cor. 12:26)

If one member suffers, all suffer with it; if one be in
honor, all rejoice with it.

I have little care for sermons written by 17<sup>th</sup> century imperialist
Christian politicians but for these occasional little quips. It is,
perhaps, a thing belonging more to sermons than it is to the time
or the people. Here, we see in Winthrop's words an idea that has
wrapped around itself within my mind and formed itself into a
new take on clades and family and life sys-side as a whole, these
last eight years.

We are one body, the Ode clade. We are one body and we each
of us Odists are members thereof. We do indeed rejoice together,
mourn together, labor and suffer together, do we not?

We may hate that at times. We may loathe that we be thus
united and we may resent that we must make each others' con-
ditions our own. We have proven that to ourselves most assid-
uously over the years, for the clade has fractured in ways large
and small.

And yet, we are still one body. We are still all of us Michelle
Hadje who was Sasha. We are still all of us connected, and if one
of us suffers, all of us suffer with them, for even if we may wear
some smug smile of satisfaction that one of our dearly beloathèd
is in pain, such resentment is a suffering.

Imagine such on the scale of the System, though! All of us
members of one body! 2.3 trillion of us live here, and we are
all beholden to the same piece of hardware, the same Dreamer
dreaming us all in all of our love and all of our stupid, petty little
squabbles that make us who we are–

I have gotten carried away. The Sightwright suffered as I do, as The Oneirotect does, and perhaps even as The Woman did, and so we all suffered with them, and the fallout of their loss is with us still.

**Page 108**   *With art comes fear.*

I had originally intended referencing I book I used for a season when teaching, *Art & Fear* by David Bayles and Ted Orland, and even shaped the words I truly spoke that day to fit. On rereading, however, I came across the first sentence of chapter 2: "Those who would make art might well begin by reflecting on the fate of those who preceded them: most who began, quit." It was at this point that I had to stop reading and pace anxiously the fields behind our cluster of townhouses, watering with tears the thirsty grasses.

**Page 121**   *Why do birds, as the poet says, suddenly appear [...]*

Cf. The Carpenters:

> Why do birds suddenly appear,
> ev'ry time you are near?
> Just like me,
> they long to be
> close to you

> Why do stars fall down from the sky,
> ev'ry time you walk by?
> Just like me,
> they long to be
> close to you

**Page 121**   [...] *...that sweet field arrayed in living green* [...]

Cf. Samuel Stennett:

> Oh, the transporting, rapturous scene
> That rises to my sight!
> Sweet fields arrayed in living green,
> And rivers of delight!

And yet, considering the role the climate crisis played in making the System our own little heaven, consider also a later verse:

> No chilling winds or poisonous breath
> Can reach that healthful shore;
> Sickness and sorrow, pain and death,
> Are felt and feared no more.

But, ah–! I will doubtless speak more on the System as heaven to come...


**Page 128**   [...] *a Blakean energetic hell.*

From Blake:

> Without contraries is no progression. Attraction and repulsion, reason and energy, love and hate, are necessary to human existence.

> From these contraries spring what the religious call Good and Evil. Good is the passive that obeys reason; Evil is the active springing from Energy.

**Page 130**   [...] *some scene, some dream within a dream within a dream* [...]
Cf. Slow Hours:

**To — in the days after her death**

A dream within a dream within a dream
and fell visions sidling up too close
both woo me. Sweet caramel and soft cream
sit cloying on their tongues, and I, Atropos
to such dreams as these, find shears on golden
          thread.

I would not cut, nor even could, had I but wished
to sever this golden thread — and every thread
is golden — and end a friend and send to mist
and sorrow ones so dear. Dead! Dead! She is dead
and gone, for her own shears were sharper still.

And so she cut, and so they watched, and so I
          watched
such love as this cease. I yearn to say that she re-
          turned
to me, became a part of me, but a tally notched
among the lost was all that stayed when life was
          spurned
by the call of death — supposedly ended.

So, she is gone and now our lives are darker for it,
and now this world is where the shadows lie,
and all the light that still remains is forfeit,
and so much green still stabs towards the sky,
and yellowed teeth of lions still snap at the air.


**Page 132**    *She passed, perhaps, the setting sun*

Cf. Emily Dickinson:

> Because I could not stop for Death —
> He kindly stopped for me —
> The Carriage held but just Ourselves —
> And Immortality.
>
> We slowly drove — He knew no haste
> And I had put away
> My labor and my leisure too,
> For His Civility —
>
> We passed the School, where Children strove
> At Recess — in the Ring —
> We passed the Fields of Gazing Grain —
> We passed the Setting Sun —
>
> Or rather — He passed Us —
> The Dews drew quivering and Chill —
> For only Gossamer, my Gown —
> My Tippet — only Tulle —

We paused before a House that seemed
A Swelling of the Ground —
The Roof was scarcely visible —
The Cornice — in the Ground —

Since then — 'tis Centuries — and yet
Feels shorter than the Day
I first surmised the Horses' Heads
Were toward Eternity —


**Page 133**   [...] *that has been my dream.*

I have dreamed of turning into a tree for years and years and
years and years and years, now.

For instance, I have written here I have set this dream into
verse and this is true, for here is a segment from a longer work:

We'd long since stopped, there by the pond,
and your smile was, yes, sad, but still fond
as you settled down wordlessly to your knees,
took a slow breath, looked out to the trees,
and closed your eyes.

Beginnings are such delicate times
and I very nearly missed it, no chimes
to announce the hour of your leaving.
As it was, there was no time for believing
or not in the next moments.

Your fingers crawled beneath the soil
and sprouted roots, flesh starting to roil.

Coarse bark spiraled up your wrists and arms,
Spelling subtle incantations and charms
to the chaos of growth.

You bowed your head and from your crown
sprouted a tender shoot covered in fine down,
soon followed by crenelated leaves and fine stems.
The pace was fast, implacable, and leaves like gems
soon arched skyward.

You sprouted and grew, taking root
in one smooth motion, fixed and mute.
Your clothing fell away, rotting in fast-time.
Naked now, you sat still, committing one last crime
of indecency.

Your face, your face! In your face was such peace
as I'd never seen, even as you gave up this lease
on life, echoed also in my heart of hearts.
I did not cry out, nor even speak, witnessing such
     arts
as your final display showed.

Soon, you were consumed, transformed as a whole.
Your head a crown of leaves, your heart a bole
bored in rough bark and sturdy wood,
your fingers, knees, and toes stood
as thirsty roots.

I stood a while by the tree that was you,

then sat at your roots and thought of all I knew
about time, transformation, death and change.
I thought about you, your life, your emotional
        range,
your gentle apotheosis.


I have also written here that I put this dream into prose, and this
is also true, for here is a segment from a short story:


> And finally, the mirroring was broken as the *her* that
> was not her slid *her* fingers up over her wrist and
> gently guided her hand down toward the soil, loamy
> and damp, and she knew then that she must spread
> her fingers and dig them down into the earth, there
> by the stairs which were a finger pointing at God
> such that she was in turn pointing at...at what? At
> the owner of that hand? At the owner of that finger?
>
> And as she did so, she felt that the dirt beneath
> her fingernails took root, that her nails themselves
> must have been rootlets and that her arm a stolon,
> that her whole body was the runner for some tree,
> some entity other than herself, for at that point, she
> took root.
>
> And her fingers crawled beneath the soil, and drank
> of the water there, and tasted the nutrients, and
> found purchase beneath the layer of loam and hu-
> mus.

And there, her fingers curled around the God-stone, and indeed, she knew it as she felt it, amber with a kernel of pain embedded within.

And even as the bark crawled up her arm, she saw her Doppelgänger stand and smile to her. A dreamy smile; not kind, not cruel, not knowing, not ignorant. Just a dreamy, inevitable smile.

And she felt growth accelerate as, bound now to the earth, her bones became wood and her muscles loosened, unwound, and thus unbound began to lengthen, to strengthen, to arch skyward, seeking stars, seeking God.

Do I repeat myself? Very well, I repeat myself. I am beholden to my dreams.

And yet! And yet, when writing the final chapter, even through the heat of the moment and the blood rushing in my ears, I began to feel within a flush of embarrassment. How indulgent it is to share this again! How indulgent, my friends, to let the dream take me again that it might shape my words! Even as I wrote, even as I cried, sitting at my desk (or trying to!), sobbing in front of my words, I struggled with feeling like this was somehow *too* indulgent.

I strive still to stifle that puritanical worrywart within, even so many years on.


**Page 134**  [...] *and so we live within a fractally cyclical tangle of time* Another perpetual theme that holds me in its claws. I wrote in an essay:

234

A year spirals up.

A day, a week, a month, they all spiral, for any one Sunday is like the previous and the next shall be much the same, but the you who experiences the differing Sundays is different. It is a spiral, proceeding steadfastly onward. A day is a spiral, with each morning much the same as the one before and the one after. A month, following the cycle of the moon.

But a year, in particular, spirals up. It carries embedded within it a certain combination of pattern, count, and duration that delineates our lives better than any other cyclical unit of time. Yes, a day is divided into night, day, and those liminal dusks and dawns, but there are so many of them. There are so many days in a life, and there are so many in a year that to see the spiral within them does not come as easily.

Our years are delineated by the seasons, though, and the count of them is so few, and the duration long enough that we can run up against that first scent of snow late in the autumn and immediately be kicked down one level of the spiral in our memories. What were we doing the last time we smelled that non-scent? What about the time before?

Or perhaps one thinks across the spiral. One, stuck in Winter, thinks back to Summer — ah, such warmth! — and tries to remember what it was one was doing then. "Only silhouettes show / in the billowing snow," Dwale writes. "Remembering months, now / gone when new blooms would grow."

And I wrote in a story:

Lyut lives his life in prayer and devotion. It is a life that is lived ascending in a steady spiral of years, for time moves upward and yet is echoed below by the change of days, the change of weeks, the change of seasons. This year, this day, this soft spring is an echo of last soft spring beneath it. It is antipodal to the autumn that will come

Cycles within cycles, spirals within spirals. This morning, too, is an echo of the day beneath it, behind it, in the past. His days are defined by the cycle of incense, prayer, fishing, foraging, meditating. He knows that it is day when he wakes when he feels the warmth from the sun. He knows when it is night when he feels the warmth fade. He knows when it is morning because he hears the birds sing. He knows that it is night when the birdsong of the day settles into the chorus of insects.

And on citing these, I am realizing just how much I am built up of obsessions, of rituals and ideas that cleave and cling and stick and meld.

**Page 138**   *[...] perhaps columbines perhaps nasturtiums [...]*

The Musician shared with me a letter and My Friend several journal entries, but, ah–! If I share them here, I will fall once more to crying. You may find them in their entirety in *Marsh*, a work written by a braver me.

I will say, however, that that letter surrounded nasturtiums and was written the night Muse quit, and those diary entries were written by My Friend, a recounting of Beckoning's memories, to comfort The Musician in her grief.

**Page 141**    (quoted directly)

From Psalm 13:2–4:

> How long, *Adonai*, will You forget me always?
>> How long hide Your face from me?
> How long shall I cast about for counsel,
>> sorrow in my heart all day?
>>> How long will my enemy loom over me?
> Regard, answer me, *HaShem*, my God.
>> Light up my eyes, lest I sleep death.

**Page 142**    (quoted directly)

From Qohelet (Ecclesiastes) 1:17:

> And I set my heart to know wisdom and to know revelry and folly, for this, too, is a herding of the wind.

From Qohelet 2:22:

> What gain is there for man in all his toil that he toils under the sun?

From Qohelet 3:20:

> Everything was from the dust, and everything goes
> back to the dust.

**Page 148**   *The blood of deer ripped to shreds by wolves!*

Cf. Czesław Miłosz:

> wystarczy pozwolić człowiekowi
> wytruć swój rodzaj
> a nastąpią niewinne wschody słońca
> nad florą i fauną wyzwoloną
>
> na pofabrycznych pustkowiach
> wyrosną dębowe lasy
> krew rozszarpanego przez wilki jelenia
> nie będzie przez nikogo widziana
> jastrząb będzie spadać na zająca
> bez świadków
>
> zniknie ze świata zło
> kiedy zniknie świadomość

×

> Simply let mankind
> extinguish itself
> And then innocent sunrises will illuminate
> liberated flora and fauna

Oak forests will grow
on postindustrial wastelands
The blood of a deer ripped apart by wolves
will not be seen by anyone
A hawk will fall, unwitnessed,
upon a rabbit

Evil will disappear from the world
once consciousness does

**Page 158**  *Do you see now the connection?*

Cf. Rilke:

> Weißt du's *noch* nicht? Wirf aus den Armen die Leere
> zu den Räumen hinzu, die wir atmen; vielleicht daß
>     die Vögel
> die erweiterte Luft fühlen mit innigerm Flug.

×

> Do you not understand *yet?* Fling from your arms the
>     emptiness
> into the spaces we breathe. It may be that the birds
> will feel the expanded air in more spirited flight.

And yet I had also in mind the cadence of Nabokov: "Give me now your full attention." A plea that one be understood.

I am no poet, but I will not deny the utility in verse when it comes to scratching the itch of words:

Give me now your full attention.

                                        I can't tell you how
I knew — but I did know that I had crossed
The border. Everything I loved was lost
But no aorta could report regret.
A sun of rubber was convulsed and set;
And blood-black nothingness began to spin
A system of cells interlinked within
Cells interlinked within cells interlinked
Within one stem. And dreadfully distinct
Against the dark, a tall white fountain played.

And here am I within a System of selves interlinked within selves
interlinked within selves interlinked within one dream.

**Page 159**  *Minutes are paragraphs of weal or woe.*

The words of John Winthrop (page 225) come once more to mind.

**Page 160**  *Not yet, though. Not this year, I suspect not this decade,
and I hope not even this century.*

I speak, of course, of functional immortality and the balm it provides against the fears artists of old faced. Keats has it:

When I have fears that I may cease to be
    Before my pen has glean'd my teeming brain,
Before high-piled books, in charact'ry,
    Hold like rich garners the full-ripen'd grain;
When I behold, upon the night's starr'd face,
    Huge cloudy symbols of a high romance,

240

And think that I may never live to trace
   Their shadows, with the magic hand of chance;
And when I feel, fair creature of an hour!
   That I shall never look upon thee more,
Never have relish in the faery power
   Of unreflecting love!—then on the shore
Of the wide world I stand alone, and think,
Till Love and Fame to nothingness do sink.


**Page 190**   *[...] perhaps like those leaves that skitter within the city, that unreal city [...]*

Cf. Charles Baudelaire via T.S. Eliot:

> *Fourmillante cité, cité pleine de rêves,*
> *Où le spectre en plein jour raccroche le passant.*

X

> Unreal city, city full of dreams,
> Where ghosts in broad daylight cling to passsers-by.


**Page 190**   *She, then, like so many leaves [...]*

Cf. Robert Graves:

> She, then, like snow in a dark night
> Fell secretly.

**Page 190**    *That unfalling ones are trapped within that last falling!*
Cf. Richard Threadgall:

> Tell to me the secret life of birds.
> No solicitors of the hungry sky are they;
> No, nor is the rainwater parting head a bookhouse
>        dialect,
> Or antiquary
> But says, "I am citizen to the eternal now,
> Republic builder of unfalling ones."
> Bound to remembering blood and numbered suns,
> What speech do we give him from our earthy fur-
>        row?
> That he has no history who has feared no pain?
> That ev'ry bird who falls with broken wing
> Halts summary in the stone that breaks his brain–
> That unfalling ones are trapped in that last falling?
> What stale rejoinders birds are unmoored with!
> The unsuffering sky exhales them in a breath.

**Page 191**    *"Oh! Oh, I do believe this is some plentiful enough for me."*

Cf. Rilke:

> Und plötzlich in diesem mühsamen Nirgends, plöt-
>        zlich
> die unsägliche Stelle, wo sich das reine Zuwenig
> unbegreiflich verwandeldt—, umspringt
> in jenes leere Zuviel.
> Wo die vielstellige Rechnung
> zahlenlos aufgeht.

×

> And suddenly in this toilsome nowhere, suddenly
> the unutterable place where the merely too little
> inscrutably mutates—, swings round
> into that empty too much,
> where the calculation to many digits
> comes out number-less.

One imagines that a 'plentiful enough' lies at some theoretical midpoint on this limitless scale from 'merely too little' to 'empty too much'. One imagines it a place just outside that 'toilsome nowhere': perhaps it sits just outside that scale, as, I fear, I hope, The Woman sits now outside the scale running from joy to suffering, having relinquished such dichotomies and embraced them—become them!—in equal measure.

I *have* to imagine it! I have to imagine that Lagrange, the System, our embedded world is plentifully enough, and not some empty too much, not after so much loss, lest I engage too readily with the fleetingness of us, a perhaps futility, a spending of time in a toilsome nowhere. Thoughts spinning out into that nowhere, crammed into a too little, emptying with a burst into some too much...

**Page 191**   [...] *breathe in a million billion trillion years* [...]

Cf. E. E. Cummings:

> i put him all into my arms
> and staggered banged with terror through
> a million billion trillion stars.

Cf. Slow Hours:

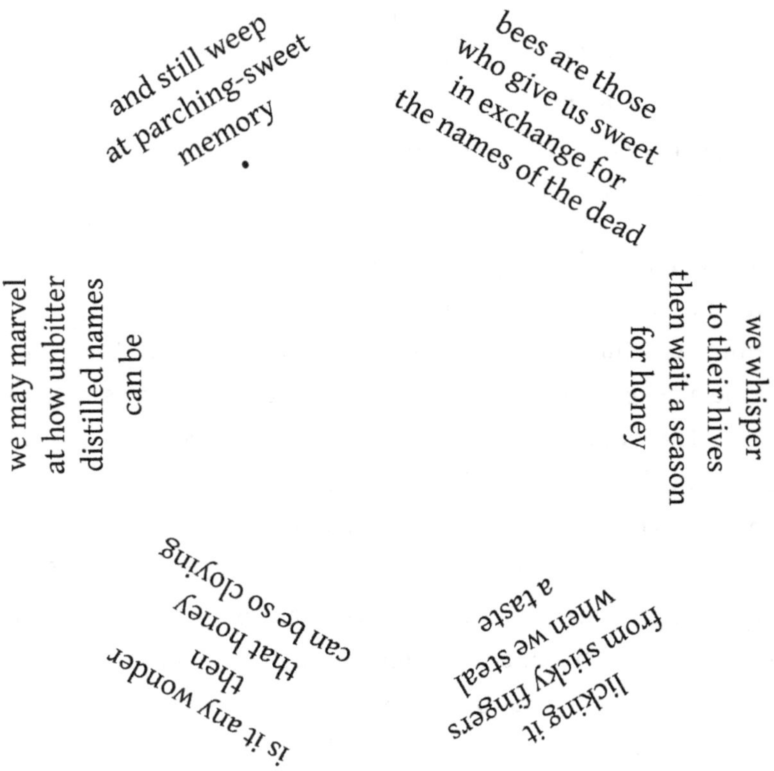


**Page 207**    ×

I used for this work a multiplication sign (×) for the section dividers, and, my dear friends, I am still coming to terms with this decision.

There are so many possible meanings!

Are we together, The Woman and I, multiplied? When she and I, when her story and mine, are intermingled, is it some greater story? My lovely readers, I hope so! I really do. I really hope, of course, that my myriad interruptions bear their own meaning and add to the whole of things, that we together are greater than the sum of the parts. I doubt and I hope in equal measure.

Are we crossed? Do we as ideas lay across each other perpendicularly? The Woman fell into stillness and I fall still through eternal, jittery, restless movement. The woman set aside her agency, in the end, and I strive for any sense of control over myself, my language, my words and sentences and paragraphs and stories. We are diametrically opposed in so many ways. We cross each other, our paths cross each other's, we approached at a ninety degree angle, and, in the end, departed at such an angle.

Are we set beside each other as some fictional love? Some two characters set within fan fiction who love each other in a way pure or unchaste in others' minds, star-crossed? Do I love her? Do I love The Woman? Did she love me?

I do not know, my dear readers. I do not know these things and I do not know many more.

Perhaps, though, perhaps it stands for that final decision: × marks the point at which I made up my mind. It is the role I played in letting The Woman, that beautiful soul who bestowed a blessing with every smile, step away from the world, for removing those blessings from us, that beauty from us, that life, that veil.

I am so, so incredibly sorry, and also rather proud of what I have done, of helping The Woman in so noble an endeavor, in equal measure.

# Appendix II — The Ode to the End of Death

*Here is the final letter that we received from our superlative friend whose memory is a blessing, including the Ode to the End of Death, those words which form our names.*

×

Sasha,

I am, in a way, leaving you with a burden. I know this, and I apologize for doing so. I do not ask for nor deserve forgiveness. The only thing I can ask for is that you remember me.

The world within was a nightmare. I am sure that you know some of what I mean. It was a nightmare and I would not wish it on anyone, and yet now, to be without it is to be incomplete. I was changed in there. We were all changed in there. You do not deny that you were not, after all. Cicero certainly was not. None of the lost came away unscathed, even if we awoke hale and hardy.

We lost Cicero, and then we *truly* lost him. The nothing that he experienced in there, the void which contained all his power

247

transmuted into weakness, the way his anger coiled about and turned back around on himself did him in in the end.

And I will not deny that the same has crossed my mind. There was a scent of the void in there, and it was alluring. I have been tempted to follow in his footsteps and seek that void out in some coarser, purer form. I decided against it. Truly decided: I made a conscious decision to stick around.

I did it for STT at first, but integrating with the theater was too stark a reminder. Then I did it for you and Priscilla, but then she passed. Then I did it for you and...well, here is where I do not deserve forgiveness. I welcome your anger, should it come, as that is perhaps what I deserve. It is not that you are not in some way worth sticking around for, as you certainly are. You have always been my champion and friend.

It is just that the call is too strong.

I have volunteered for an early procedure. A way back. Or, rather, a way to a new place. A way to be embedded within a system, rather than simply within a hall of mirrors. I cannot say where, other than it is not in the Western Fed. All I can tell you is that the world should expect big things when it comes to what we have learned from the lost.

I will not say that there is no chance that we may some day meet again. My body will die, I am told, but should my mind and my sense of self miraculously survive, then I will be on my own once more. This time, however, it will be my choice.

There will be those who come after. Perhaps *you* will come after. Perhaps you will yearn for that return to the eternal dream where memory does not die. And maybe those who come after will do so for other reasons, but they will come.

Should I survive and then others come after, perhaps I will meet them. But it is best to assume that I will not. Maybe it is best to think of it as a sort of suicide, in the end. Here I am, going off to find a better place, and doing so through death. A place that is inaccessible to you or anyone, except perhaps some anonymous scientist in a lab, typing at a terminal.

If I see you again, I will greet you with open arms. If I do not, know that I loved you to the last, in my own way.

I have little else to offer but the imperfect words that plagued me while I was lost.

> I am at a loss for images in this end of days:
> I have sight but cannot see.
> I build castles out of words;
> I cannot stop myself from speaking.
> I still have will and goals to attain,
> I still have wants and needs.
> And if I dream, is that not so?
> If I dream, am I no longer myself?[1]
> If I dream, am I still buried beneath words?
> And I still dream even while awake.
>
> Life breeds life, but death must now be chosen[2]
> for memory ends at the teeth of death.
> The living know that they will die,
> but the dead know nothing.
> Hold my name beneath your tongue and know:

---

[1] Z"L

[2] Z"L. Later known as Qoheleth, whose story is told in Ioan Bălan's *On the Perils of Memory*, later published under the title *Qoheleth*.

when you die, thus dies the name.
To deny the end is to deny all beginnings,
and to deny beginnings is to become immortal,
and to become immortal is to repeat the past,
which cannot itself, in the end, be denied.

Oh, but to whom do I speak these words?
To whom do I plead my case?
From whence do I call out?
What right have I?
No ranks of angels will answer to dreamers,
No unknowable spaces echo my words.
Before whom do I kneel, contrite?
Behind whom do I await my judgment?
Beside whom do I face death?
And why wait I for an answer?

Among those who create are those who forge:
Moving ceaselessly from creation to creation.
And those who remain are those who hone,
Perfecting singular arts to a cruel point.
To forge is to end, and to own beginnings.
To hone is to trade ends for perpetual perfection.
In this end of days, I must begin anew.
In this end of days, I seek an end.
In this end of days, I reach for new beginnings
that I may find the middle path.

Time is a finger pointing at itself
that it might give the world orders.
The world is an audience before a stage
where it watches the slow hours progress.
And we are the motes in the stage-lights,
Beholden to the heat of the lamps.
If I walk backward, time moves forward.
If I walk forward, time rushes on.
If I stand still, the world moves around me,
and the only constant is change.

Memory is a mirror of hammered silver:
a weapon against the waking world.
Dreams are the plate-glass atop memory:
a clarifying agent that reflects the sun.
The waking world fogs the view,
and time makes prey of remembering.
I remember sands beneath my feet.
I remember the rattle of dry grass.
I remember the names of all things,
and forget them only when I wake.

If I am to bathe in dreams,
then I must be willing to submerge myself.
If I am to submerge myself in memory,
then I must be true to myself.
If I am to always be true to myself,
then I must in all ways be earnest.
I must keep no veil between me and my words.

I must set no stones between me and my actions.
I must show no hesitation when speaking my name,
for that is my only possession.

The only time I know my true name is when I
      dream.[3]
The only time I dream is when need an answer.
Why ask questions, here at the end of all things?
Why ask questions when the answers will not help?
To know one's true name is to know god.
To know god is to answer unasked questions.
Do I know god after the end waking?
Do I know god when I do not remember myself?
Do I know god when I dream?
May then my name die with me.

That which lives is forever praiseworthy,
for they, knowing not, provide life in death.
Dear the wheat and rye under the stars:
serene; sustained and sustaining.
Dear, also, the tree that was felled[4]
which offers heat and warmth in fire.
What praise we give we give by consuming,
what gifts we give we give in death,

---

[3] Now known as Sasha after the events told in Ioan Bălan's *Individuation & Reconciliation*, later published under the title *Mitzvot*. I will write her a *zikhrona livracha*, here, as she who is True Name is no more, not as she was, and to her, to so many of us, this, too, is a death.

[4] No longer with us here on Lagrange. A loss is a loss is a loss; may its memory be a blessing.

what lives we lead we lead in memory,
and the end of memory lies beneath the roots.

May one day death itself not die?[5]
Should we rejoice in the end of endings?
What is the correct thing to hope for?
I do not know, I do not know.[6]
To pray for the end of endings
is to pray for the end of memory.[7]
Should we forget the lives we lead?
Should we forget the names of the dead?
Should we forget the wheat, the rye, the tree?[8]
Perhaps this, too, is meaningless.

May this be the end of death. Failing that, may the memory of me die and be food for the growth of those who come after.

Yours always,

AwDae

---

[5] *Z"L*

[6] *Z"L*

[7] Shall I write here that her name, in death, is a blessing? Does she get her own *zikhrona livracha?* I do not know, friends, but I will say that, yes, her memory *is* a blessing, regardless of whether or not she still lives.

[8] *Z"L*

# IDUMEA. C.M.

"A time to be born and a time to die." — ECCL. 3:2

Chas. Wesley, 1753.   Key of A Minor.                    A. Davidson, 1817.

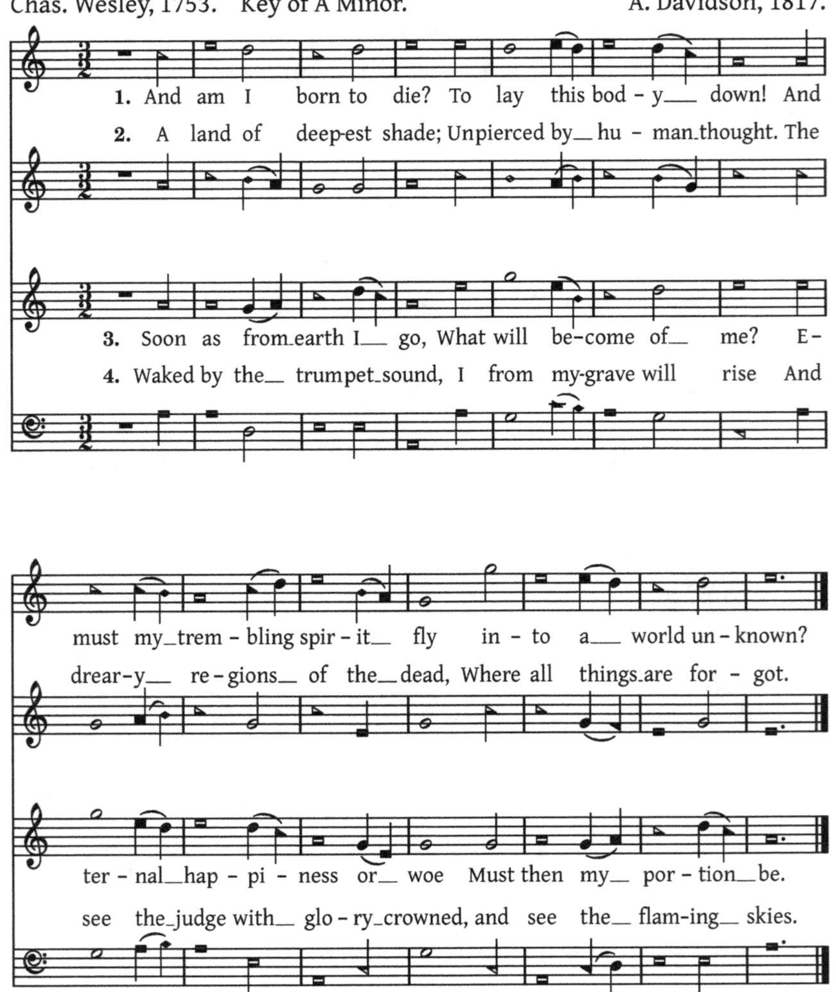

# Appendix III — The hymn "Idumea"

*Idumea* is named after a hymn by A. Davidson with words by Charles Wesley, published in *Sacred Tunes and Hymns: Containing a Special Collection of a Very High Order of Standard Sacred Tunes and Hymns Novel and Newly Arranged* by J. S. James in 1913. Idumea itself refers to Edom—unless, perhaps, you are Blake and think that "Now is the dominion of Edom, and the return of Adam into Paradise" refers to us!—a kingdom in the Ancient Near East. While this has little to do with the story told within, it does sound rather pleasing to the ear, does it not? And so does the hymn, at that. The hollowness of the song with all its open fifths, the raw, coarse beauty that comes with Sacred Harp singing, the beat of the tactus and the ache of the singers hollering out words that nearly yearn for death are what led to the title of this book.

Or, as a friend said upon learning of this project, ""Main character escaping suffering while the narrator stays stuck in it" is somewhat analogous to living singers singing songs almost exclusively about how great it will be to die and escape from suffering"—which, as a quote, is quite painful to go back and read for your humble narrator, as I am sure you can imagine.

The hymn is reproduced here for reference. Despite being

in short meter, the typo of it being in common meter ('C.M.') is retained from its original printing.

# Appendix IV — Reading



×

All readings are the same. They all begin the same way, with stepping off to some sim, known or unknown, where she would arrive a good hour early. There, she would wait or walk or drink her coffee or tea. Would it be a bookshop this time? Would it be a library? Would she run her fingerpads along the spines of books, counting known and unknown titles?

Perhaps it was a cafe, and she would get herself a little pastry, some crumbly thing to eat while wandering lazily outside or inspecting the various pieces of art lining the walls within.

She would get there an hour early and simply inhabit the space.

As time drew closer, as her contact would come out to meet her, she would feel the excitement begin to prickle at the back of her neck, and she would have to restrain herself from letting her hackles raise or her tail bristle out. Some long-forgotten and perhaps-imagined reaction to danger tickling both human and skunk parts of her mind. She would feel her scalp tingle and her tail threaten to hike, and she would sit in that sensation. She would bathe in it. She would relish every shift of every strand of fur, and as she sat, legs crossed and coffee or water cradled in her lap, listening to her contact chatter, she would delight in the nervous anticipation of the reading to come.

"Will you be reading from a physical copy or an exo?"

"Oh, an exo," she said, smiling. "As much love as I hold for the physical tools of the trade, I hold yet more for all of the tools at our disposal. Especially when they let me be more dramatic."

They laughed. "Right, you were an actor before, yeah?"

She nodded. "Of a sort, yes."

"And how long will your reading be?"

"I have a variety of segments prepared, from five minutes to an hour."

They blinked. "An hour? Holy shit."

She shrugged gracefully, smile still lingering on her muzzle. "Perhaps another artifact of being an actor. I could talk the ears off a fox."

Laughter.

"Shall we aim for somewhere in the middle? Twenty minutes, perhaps?"

"That'll work, yeah. You're the only slot, tonight, but that'll still give you at least forty minutes for Q&A." They smirked, adding, "Which I imagine you'll need. I read your book, by the way."

It was her turn to laugh, musical and joyous. "I am pleased to hear! I trust that you have questions of your own?"

"Oh, *plenty.*"

"Delightful," she said, clapping her paws together. "I shall look forward to them, then."

This conversation echoed a hundred times, a thousand, in her memories. This conversation and so many others like it set the stage. This conversation and so many others like it became one of the steps in that liminal space between the waking world and the dream of her stories.

She would step away from home or from a meeting or from a cocladist's and at that moment, at the precise instant she ceased being *there* and started being *here,* she was in a place between. She was in a time between times and a world between worlds.

She dwelt, then, in the world of the Ode. She knew where it was from, her name. Not just the Ode itself, but the place the line itself referenced. She had talked to the poet in her own way—perhaps it was closer to prayer, but she bothered not with distinctions such as these—and she knew the scene ey had been painting. She knew that ey had sat at the edge of the natural area some few blocks away from their high school, sat on the fencepost and looked out east, out beyond the natural area and wind farm to where the coarse shortgrass prairie dissolved into rectilinear fields. Tan, perhaps, or brown or gray, they would all shine the same beneath the moon, beneath the stars. They were all dear to em. They were all dear to *her.*

So as soon as she would step away from home and before she would step up to the lectern, she would dwell there at the edge of the natural space. There is where she would feel her hackles threaten to rise and her tail threaten to bristle. She would look at the art and see nothing. She would drink her coffee or tea or eat her pastry and it would have a flavor she did not experience.

She would have her conversations on autopilot, and her earnest smile would be no less earnest for her absence from the space. She would do all of these things and overlaid atop her vision would be fields silvered by starlight. She would do all of these things and her tongue would be coated with the taste of sweet night air, of dust and pollen and petrichor. She would strain to hear her contact through the soft noises of wind and crickets.

And then, with all the suddenness of dawn, a chorus of birdsong crashing through her mind, the moment would come. Her contact would stand before the gathered crowd and introduce her—her! Dear The Wheat And Rye Under The Stars! She was published! She was an author! The realization would never not startle her—and she would brush out her tail one last time, run her fingers through her mane, and step out of the liminal space of the Ode and into the dream of her story. The nervous excitement would wash away and she would be *here*. She would be *now*.

And then she would read.

# Acknowledgments

Thanks is due first of all to Jacob Geller, who knows me not, for he created a video on the story of Pinocchio that touched me so deeply that I began this project in the first place. Thanks also to Tomash and Yule, who contributed so much to this story; it would not be what it is without them. To Isiat, adoration for his boundless support. To barnaby on the Apocrypals Discord for help with Sacred Harp hymns. To Mae and Taija and Andréa C. Mason for reminding me that my work is indeed read. Finally, I will forever sing the praises of my polycule and those within for their support and love, and for the privilege of loving them in turn.

*Idumea* was funded by a Kickstarter campaign. These are those who brought it to fruition:

**Krzysztof "Tomash" Drewniak, Andréa CERES Mason,** *Alexandria Christina Leal, Nathan Merrifield, Taija, Fiona Adams, Stephen Moore, Xideron, Ashley Hale,* Amdusias, Fén Cupit, ramshackle heather, doctorlit, nova, Ash Holland, Michael Miele, Webster Leone, Clover Arizona, Aulden Stargazer, raine, Astra Jones, David Scoggins, Rachel Dillon. Charles S. Petrov Neutrino, Chandler Hines, Royce Day, Isiat, Craig, ubuntor, Joel Kreissman, Sethvir, Barac Baker Wiley.

# About the authors

Madison Rye Progress, like your humble narrator, is also struck by graphomania. She is one to wake at all hours and sneak off to her computer or take notes on her phone or simply pace the quiet rooms of her house, lonely, building worlds in her head. She sought relief from the Furry Writers' Guild, from the Regional Anthropomorphic Writers' Retreat with Kyell Gold and Dayna Smith, but they only encouraged her. She sought relief from Cornell college, but they only gave her an MFA in creative writing and pedagogy. She sought relief in her love, *Samantha Yule Fireheart,* who lives with her in the Pacific Northwest, but they instead spend their days writing with each other, as does she with the Post-Self community, where she met *Krzysztof "Tomash" Drewniak* and where she curates the canon.

She, too, wonders if she is born to die. What, dear readers, will become of her? What will become of her? What will become of her? What will become of her? What will become of her? What will become of her? What will become of her? What will become of her? And is she born to die? What will become of her? And is she born to die? What will become of her? What will become of her? What will become of her? What will become of her? What will become of her? What will become of her?

Madison Rye Progress
**makyo.ink**

Samantha Yule Fireheart
**everdream.space**

Krzysztof "Tomash" Drewniak
**kdrewniak.com**